THE BALFOUR BRIDES

A proud, powerful dynasty...

Scandal has rocked the core of the infamous
Balfour family...

Its glittering, gorgeous daughters are in disgrace.

Banished from the Balfour mansion, they're sent to
the boldest, most magnificent men in the world to be
wedded, bedded...and tamed!

And so begins a scandalous saga of dazzling
glamour and passionate surrender.

**Each month, Harlequin Presents®
is delighted to bring you an exciting new
installment from THE BALFOUR BRIDES.
You won't want to miss out!**

Eight volumes to collect and treasure!

Emily had the sensation of standing on a track in the path of a speeding train, knowing that the moment of impact was almost upon her. He wouldn't recognize her, she reassured herself desperately. Why would he? They'd only met once—and then only for a couple of minutes in a situation that was a world away from this. He must meet thousands of women...*kiss thousands of women...*

Someone was speaking. "This is one of the valuable volunteers who bring new experiences into the lives of our young people. Miss Jones is a graduate of the Royal School of Ballet..."

Like an automaton Emily bent her head and sank down in a curtsy. From an etiquette point of view it was the right thing to do, but more importantly it also gave her a great chance to avoid looking up at the man she'd last seen in the garden at Balfour, when he'd drawn her into the shadow of the trees and kissed her with an arrogance and an expertise that shocked and thrilled and horrified her.

Call me when you grow up...

She steeled herself, and looked up.

The express train hit. For a moment the breath was knocked out of her and it was like falling. Like skydiving into the sunset. And then realizing that you didn't have a parachute.

Luis Cordoba raised one fine eyebrow a fraction. Beneath it his eyes were a hard, dull gold. "Really, Miss *Jones?*"

India Grey

EMILY AND THE
NOTORIOUS PRINCE

The Balfour Brides

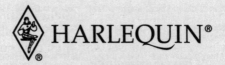

HARLEQUIN®

TORONTO • NEW YORK • LONDON
AMSTERDAM • PARIS • SYDNEY • HAMBURG
STOCKHOLM • ATHENS • TOKYO • MILAN • MADRID
PRAGUE • WARSAW • BUDAPEST • AUCKLAND

Special thanks and acknowledgment are given to
India Grey for her contribution to
The Balfour Brides series.

Recycling programs
for this product may
not exist in your area.

ISBN-13: 978-0-373-12946-1

EMILY AND THE NOTORIOUS PRINCE

First North American Publication 2010.

Copyright © 2010 by Harlequin Books S.A.

All about the author...
India Grey

A self-confessed romance junkie, **INDIA GREY** was just thirteen years old when she first sent off for the Harlequin® writers' guidelines. She can still recall the thrill of getting the large brown envelope with its distinctive logo through the letterbox, and subsequently whiled away many a dull school day staring out of the window and dreaming of the perfect hero. She kept these guidelines with her for the next ten years, tucking them carefully inside the cover of each new diary in January, and beginning every list of New Year's resolutions with the words *Start Novel.* In the meantime she gained a degree in English Literature and Language from Manchester University, and in a stroke of genius on the part of the Gods of Romance, met her gorgeous future husband on the very last night of their three years there. The past fifteen years have been spent blissfully buried in domesticity, and heaps of pink washing generated by three small daughters, but she has never really stopped daydreaming about romance. She's just profoundly grateful to have finally got an excuse to do it legitimately!

For the Elmhurst Olympics crowd,
and for Louise in particular; much-loved
keeper of the family flame.

xx

PROLOGUE

'*CALL* me when you grow up!'

As Emily ducked beneath the ghostly, blossom-shrouded trees and emerged onto the twilit lawn his voice followed her: mocking, amused and, with its faintly exotic accent, horribly sexy.

She quickened her pace, thinking only of putting as much distance as possible between herself and the man in the shadows. Head bent, oblivious to the curious stares of the guests scattered across the velvet lawns of Balfour Manor, she hurried towards the house, pressing her teeth down into a lip that still tingled and throbbed from where he had kissed her.

The 99th Balfour Charity Ball was in full swing and the sound of laughter, conversation and clinking glasses drifted above the music coming from the marquee. Ahead of her the majestic house shimmered with light from every window, its honey-coloured stone glowing in the dusk like old gold. Behind her the darkness of the garden pressed at her back, spreading goose bumps over her skin. Her heart was beating so hard she could feel it all through her body, a rapid, throbbing pulse that intensified as she ran lightly up the shallow stone steps to the house.

He had ruined everything.

She'd looked forward to this party for so long—all those years at boarding school, when she'd been reduced to picking over the edited details of the annual Balfour Ball in celebrity magazines and piecing together snatches of gossip from her older sisters. This year, with ballet school all but finished, her time had finally come.

She blinked as she stepped into the brightness of the hallway. Heading straight for the stairs she gathered up the long skirt of her dress, trying not to think of the excitement with which she'd put it on only a couple of hours earlier. She had felt so grown up and sophisticated…

Until the moment those knowing, gold-flecked eyes had wandered lazily over her, and then she had felt something different altogether.

Reaching her bedroom she slammed the door and leaned against it for a moment, breathing hard. The room was filled with violet shadows which blurred the edges of everything, making the familiar objects seem suddenly strange and unrecognizable. She didn't turn on the light though. Instead she found herself drawn towards the window.

Spread out before her the garden glittered with tiny lights. It was like a picture from a child's storybook—an enchanted kingdom, the butterfly ball. And that's what she'd wanted, she thought with a sob, leaning her burning forehead against the pane. She'd wanted it to be like a fairy tale, with the handsome prince just waiting to fall in love with her.

Her eyes were drawn beyond the delicate strings of fairy lights and the glittering crystal chandeliers that stood on the tables across the lawn; deeper, into the darkness itself, where inky shadows moved beneath the trees.

That's where he was.

Emily pressed her hands to the glass, suddenly pierced by a shaft of longing so pure and painful that she couldn't breathe. His cool, clean taste was still on her lips and she ran her tongue over them, remembering the moment when he had stepped out in front of her beneath the trees and pulled her to him—languidly, unhurriedly, as if it had been the most natural thing in the world…

And kissed her.

She had been too shocked to resist. It was as if some powerful tidal wave had been unleashed inside her and she was helpless to do anything as it sucked her down, into warm, secret whirlpools of unfathomable sensation, obliterating logic. His mouth moved over hers, slowly and expertly, and his fingers caressed the back of her neck, the hollow beneath her jaw, sending ripples of intense, shuddering pleasure down her spine, until she felt taut and fragile enough to shatter.

And then he lifted his head and in that moment she caught the gleam of his wicked gold eyes in the darkness. The spell was broken and she surfaced again, gasping and fighting for breath, speechless and horrified at her own unrecognisable behaviour. Terrified of the ease with which he had made her act like that.

Because Prince Luis Cordoba of Santosa was handsome, of that there was no doubt. But he wasn't interested in love, and behind the designer suit and dazzling smile he was no harmless, fairy-tale Prince Charming.

Dangerous, compelling, beguiling…

He was the wolf.

CHAPTER ONE

One year later

BALFOUR MANOR—golden and majestic and glowing like topaz in a bed of emerald velvet. Every detail was as familiar to Emily as the back of her own hand. And yet it was the last thing she expected to see in the grimy, diesel-scented chill of the underground station.

It was rush hour. Carried along in the flow of harassed and preoccupied commuters, blinking in the sudden gloom after the brightness of the May evening outside, Emily's first thought was that she was imagining it. That, after two months of self-imposed exile in a bedsit that added a whole new dimension to the word *grim*, her homesickness had finally got the better of her and she was hallucinating.

Behind her a man cannoned into her as she stopped in her tracks, and swore disgustedly. Muttering apologies Emily ducked her head and pushed against the stream of people, back in the direction of the news stand. She must have been mistaken. It was a picture of Buckingham Palace she'd seen—some story about a minor royal indiscretion or—

Illegitimacy Scandal Rocks Balfour Legacy

Light-headed with horror Emily snatched up a paper and scanned the column beneath the headline, her mind reeling. It bristled with exclamation marks and was dotted with sly ellipses, but the names jumped out at her: *Olivia Balfour... Bella... Alexandra... Zoe...*

Zoe?

'Are you going to buy that paper? I'm not running a library here, you know.'

From an alternative reality the disgruntled voice of the newspaper-seller penetrated her consciousness. 'Oh. Yes. Sorry. Of course,' she said hastily, delving into the pocket of her cardigan for the five-pound tip given to her by a drunken businessman who had told her all about his wife and kids and then put his hand up her skirt. Mollified, the newspaper man gave her a conspiratorial wink.

''Ow the other 'arf live, eh? Beautiful houses in all the best spots across the world, cars, money, parties—but I ask you, is any one of them Balfours happy?' Shaking his head, he gave an amused chuckle.

No, Emily thought numbly as she backed away, the paper clutched in her hands. *I don't think we are—not any more.* She attempted to give him an answering smile, but her face was stiff, her eyes wide and unblinking as the words from the article swooped and swelled inside her head: *shocking discovery... illicit affair...illegitimate...disgrace... scandal...*

Just a year ago it had all been so different. As she rejoined the press of people the moment before the guests started to arrive and she had gone downstairs in her blue silk dress, feeling so grown-up.

But she hadn't been grown up at all. Not then. She'd been stupidly, embarrassingly naive.

She rejoined the press of people crowding down into the airless tunnel, holding the newspaper with its lurid headline against her body as if that way she could keep its accusations and speculations secret from the rest of the world. As she waited on the platform she noticed with a stab of anguish that a woman to her left was holding a copy of the paper, her face bored and expressionless as she read the story beneath the headline, as if it was insignificant.

A rumble in the darkness indicated the arrival of the train. Pushing to the front of the crowd squeezing onto the train with uncharacteristic assertiveness, Emily slipped quickly into an empty seat, for the first time in her life without looking round to see if anyone else needed it. As the train jerked into the darkness of the tunnel she took a deep breath and unfolded the paper.

Exclusive! When Blue Blood Turns Bad

Last night there was only one place to see and be seen—at the Balfour Charity Ball! But despite the glitz and the glamour, all was not as it seemed.

Behind the scenes, Olivia Balfour and her scandalous twin Bella were locked in a battle over a shocking discovery—that their late mother, socialite Alexandra Balfour, had conceived their sister Zoe during an illicit affair!

Biting her lip against a whimper of distress Emily raised her head and stared blindly ahead of her as Zoe's face swam into her mind. Beautiful, wild Zoe, with her dazzling green eyes that set her apart from her blue-eyed sisters.

She looked down at the paper again, scanning over the rest of the article as her mind whirred and her stomach churned. She was trembling, as if she was cold, and had to grip the paper tightly in both hands to hold it steady enough to read.

The Balfour name might be synonymous with glamour and style, but this is the second illegitimate family member to be outed in as many months. It seems this dynasty is rotten to its core....

Which was more or less the same accusation that she'd hurled at her father on the night of Mia's untimely arrival at Balfour Manor. Emily stiffened as the memory of that appalling evening seized her in an icy grip. Poor Mia. She had come in search of a happy family and had instead had walked straight into a tragedy worthy of Chekhov.

The train jolted to a standstill in another station, bringing Emily roughly back to the present. She blinked, looking around her as another tide of people ebbed and flowed through the doors—anonymous faces with lives and interests and joys and heartaches she couldn't begin to guess. And she was just another of them. Another anonymous face in the crowd. A girl on her way home from work, just like any other.

A void of loneliness opened up in front of her, and before she could do anything she felt herself hurtling into it. She squeezed her eyes shut, sucking in a breath, momentarily dizzy and disorientated with homesickness. It happened from time to time; she was getting used to it. It was just a case of holding on and waiting for it to pass. The problem was, up until two months ago, her family and her dancing had been her whole life. And now she had neither.

She looked down at the newspaper, avid for any crumbs of information about the people she loved and had turned her back on so completely. At the bottom of the front page article she read: '*For a full report and pictures of last night's sparkling charity ball, see pages 12–13...*'

With shaking fingers she turned the pages, smoothing the paper across her knees as she came to the colourful splash of photographs. Tears leapt into her eyes, but she blinked them away impatiently. Oh, God, there was Kat, looking gorgeous in a dress of scarlet satin, and Bella and Olivia standing together, their dazzling, practised smiles not quite hiding the tension in their eyes. '*The calm before the cat-fight,*' read the caption beneath the picture. Looking into their familiar faces Emily realised that she was smiling, even though her heart felt like it was being prised open with a pickaxe, but her smile faded as her gaze moved to a picture of her father standing next to a familiar and distinguished English actress. She was a long-time friend of the family, but noticing the way Oscar's hand was looped lightly round her waist Emily suddenly found herself wondering if she'd ever been more than that....

The shadows gathered at the corners of her mind, the dark shapes slipping through the trees.

Hating herself for her cynicism and suspicion, hating her father for planting it in her mind, she glanced quickly away, to the next photograph.

And froze.

She tried to tear her gaze away. Really, she did. She didn't want to keep looking helplessly into the slanting golden eyes that stared straight out at her from the page, or remember how it had felt to have them looking back at her for real. Moving over her body. Glittering with amusement and delicious wickedness...

'Prince Luis Cordoba of Santosa arrives at the party,' said the text beneath the picture. *'But will the newly reformed playboy prince be able to withstand the temptation of the wild and wayward Balfour girls?'*

At that moment the train juddered to a halt and dazedly Emily realised she'd reached her stop. She sprang to her feet, bundling the paper up. For a split second she considered leaving it on the seat, but instead found herself tucking it under her arm as she got off the train.

Because she hated the thought of a stranger picking it up and poring over the sordid details of her family's disgrace, she told herself as she walked briskly towards the stairs. Not because she wanted to read any more about Luis Cordoba, or gaze longer at the photograph of him looking brooding and beautiful in black tie, for goodness' sake.

Of course not.

Why would she? He was dangerous, and Emily didn't like

danger. She had no interest in him whatsoever—a fact which she'd made perfectly clear at last year's ball.

And just to prove it to herself again now, she dropped the paper into the first bin she passed at the entrance to the station. And she allowed herself a small smile of satisfaction as she walked purposefully away.

'Where in hell's name are we, exactly?'

Luis gazed moodily out of the blacked-out window as his car nosed its way slowly through the traffic-clogged outer reaches of London. At least he assumed they were still in London, though the dingy rows of scruffy houses bore little resemblance to the elegant city he was familiar with.

His private secretary consulted his clipboard. 'I believe it's a place called Larchfield Park, sir,' he said gravely. 'It's an area with a high proportion of unemployed residents, and significant problems with drug abuse, gang violence and gun and knife crime.'

'How charming,' Luis drawled, leaning back against the soft leather upholstery with a twisted smile. 'Tomás, may I suggest that if you ever leave your job in the royal household you don't apply for a position as a holiday rep. If I'd wanted to die I could have simply crashed my helicopter into the nearest cliff in Santosa.'

Tomás didn't smile. 'Sir, please let me reassure you that the car is fully armoured. You're in no danger. Since the crown prince's death we've increased security by—'

'I know,' Luis interrupted wearily. 'I was joking. Forget it.'

He closed his eyes. His hangover, held at bay all day by a combination of strong painkillers and stronger coffee, was threatening to make a comeback, hammering at his temples with depressing persistence. He had only himself to blame, of course…

But then he was used to that.

Anyway, he thought bleakly, given that his behaviour for the past ten months had been completely exemplary, he could just about forgive himself one minor lapse at the Balfour Charity

Ball. Especially since no high-profile models had been involved. No married women. No women at all, in fact. His vow to Rico was intact. It had just been him and a rather too plentiful supply of Oscar Balfour's excellent champagne.

It was all so different from last year.

He looked out of the window, not seeing the evening sunlight slanting onto the graffiti-daubed walls, the litter-strewn streets, but a pair of blue eyes—Balfour blue, people called it—and remembering the way their clear, cornflower-coloured depths had darkened when he'd kissed her. With shock, and with desire perhaps, but also with…

Deus.

He felt a stab of self-disgust as he pushed the memory away. Perhaps it was just as well Oscar's youngest daughter hadn't been there last night. Emily Balfour had been every bit as beautiful as her older sisters—a fact which had initially distracted him from her quite astonishing lack of experience. If he'd known how green she was he would have taken it more slowly, taken more time to draw out the tremulous passion he had sensed beneath her rigidly polite veneer. But hindsight was a wonderful thing. Last year, if he'd known a lot of things that now seemed all too bloody obvious, his life would look very different.

'We're here, sir.'

Tomás's voice interrupted his thoughts and Luis realised the car had pulled into a sort of compound surrounded by high wire-mesh fencing. It was now coming to a standstill outside a shabby-looking single-storey building that had clearly seen better days.

His security team had arrived ahead of them and were attempting to be discreet as they patrolled the perimeter of the compound, while a guard stood in the doorway and talked into a microphone headset. A small crowd of gangly youths in hooded sweatshirts had gathered on the other side of the fence.

Luis sighed inwardly.

'Remind me what we're here for again?'

'Well, sir, it's a dance group of—'

Luis groaned and held up his hands. 'OK, you can stop right there, unless the next part of that sentence was going to be "eighteen-year-old exotic belly dancers".'

'No, sir.' Tomás consulted his clipboard again. 'It's mixed programme. This is a local youth centre, which provides a number of different sports and dance classes for children aged from four to sixteen. Tonight we're here to watch a performance of tap, jazz, street dance and ballet.'

'Ballet?' Luis repeated scathingly, '*Meu Deus*. I take it this is all part of the master plan to reinvent me as sincere, high-minded patron of the arts.'

'The press office did think this kind of involvement with children's community arts would be a useful way of highlighting a more sensitive side to your character, yes, sir.'

Despair and frustration closed in on Luis, surrounding him as palpably as the high wire fence against which the youths were gathering outside. 'In that case you'd better nudge me when it's time to clap,' he said wearily. 'And wake me up if I start to snore.'

Emily turned the corner from the tube station and hurried in the direction of the community centre. She was late. Across the road a cherry tree in full blossom was like a ghostly galleon in full sail in the gloom, and as she walked quickly past, a gust of sudden wind sent white petals swirling across the street, their scent for a moment overpowering the spicy smell of Indian and African food from the takeaway shops at the end of the street. Emily pulled her lumpy second-hand cardigan more tightly around her, bracing herself against another wave of homesickness as she remembered the Japanese cherry trees at the end of the rose walk at Balfour. *Where Luis Cordoba had kissed her,* a wicked little voice reminded her.

She quickened her pace, automatically lifting her hand to her mouth at the memory as if she could scrub it away, and along with it the disturbing, insistent feelings it aroused in her.

But the next moment all that was forgotten as she saw the crowd of hooded teenagers pressed against the fence of the community centre. As she got closer she could see what was drawing them: two black, official-looking cars with darkened windows were parked in front of the building.

Oh, God. Her heart plummeted and her footsteps faltered as fear seized her. What was it this time? Another stabbing? Or a shooting...

And then she was running, her heavy plait thudding against her back with every step, her eyes fixed on the scruffy building to which she had become so attached in the past two lonely months. Larchfield Youth Centre offered a refuge from the problems of the outside world and gave a new sense of purpose to the lives of hundreds of underprivileged, displaced and disillusioned young people.

And to one overprivileged, displaced and disillusioned heiress too.

A sinister-looking man was standing by the door, wearing a headset. She glanced at him nervously, half expecting him to try to stop her from going in, but he merely stared at her impassively which worried her even more somehow. Heart thudding uneasily, she hurried along the dingy corridor, breathing in the now-familiar smell of teenagers—hormones and hair gel, undercut with a faint trace of stale cigarettes—towards the girl's changing room at the far end. As she opened the door she was instantly enveloped in chatter of fifty excited voices.

In the midst of the crush of Lycra-clad girls, Kiki Odiah, Larchfield's youth worker, was spraying glittery hairspray over the head of a small girl in a silver leotard and tap shoes. Emily pushed her way over, shrugging off her bulky cardigan as she went.

'Sorry I'm late. I haven't had time to go home and change.'

Through a cloud of glitter Kiki threw her a glance of pure relief. 'You're here now, honey, that's all that matters.'

'What's going on?' Emily couldn't keep the anxiety from her

voice. 'I saw the cars outside—is it immigration? They haven't come for the Luambos, have they?'

Kiki shook her head so the beads in her hair gave a musical rattle. Her dark eyes glittered with suppressed excitement as she sprayed hairspray on the next small head. 'You'll never guess.'

'Tell me, then!'

'Royalty.'

'*What?*' Emily gasped, a chilly sensation of misgiving prickling at the base of her spine. Several of the minor royals were friends of Oscar and regular visitors to Balfour. 'Who?'

Kiki shrugged. 'Not British, that's all I know.' Luckily she was too absorbed in hairspraying to register Emily's visible relief, shaking the can with a rattle as she continued. 'But then I'm just a lowly youth worker. I only found out about all of this when a carload of men in suits arrived and started crawling over every inch of the place this afternoon. And now the whole of the council youth services department have showed up, and are suddenly taking an interest in what we do.' She rolled her eyes. 'Which is what you might call ironic, seeing as we've only got enough money to keep us open for the next two months.'

'Maybe that's why they're here, whoever they are, to give us the money to stay open?' Emily suggested hopefully. The issue of funding hung over everything at Larchfield like a guillotine.

'I don't see why. I'm no expert, but it sounds to me like these guys are talking Spanish, and I can't imagine why any Spanish royalty would be interested in giving money to Larchfield.'

Emily frowned. 'I can't imagine why Spanish royalty would be coming to watch our dance show either. I mean, the children have worked really hard, but it's hardly Sadler's Wells.'

'Search me.' Kiki looked over the children's heads to the swarthy, olive-skinned guard who had just come into the room, and giggled. 'In fact, I wish he *would* search me. I just can't resist those dark Latin types, can you?'

'Yes, as a matter of fact I can,' said Emily a little too tartly, as the image of Luis Cordoba flashed, infuriatingly, into her head. 'Especially at the moment, when we've got fifty children to get ready to go onstage in a little over fifteen minutes.'

'OK, Miss Prim and Proper!' Kiki grinned. 'You go and organise your cygnets and I'll practise my curtsy.'

And she grabbed the hands of the nearest little silver-clad tap dancer and whirled her round, singing, 'One day my prince will come,' and laughing.

All that was missing were the thumbscrews and a tuneless rendition of 'Somewhere Over the Rainbow', thought Luis as he surreptitiously slid back the starched cuff of his shirt and tried to check his watch.

Smothering a sigh he shifted position on the hard plastic chair that was way too small to accommodate his shoulders and the length of his legs. Actually, even without the thumbscrews it was a pretty effective torture. Beside him, Tomás was smiling benignly at the stage where numerous little girls dressed in silver leotards clattered chaotically through a tap routine. But, of course, Tomás had a little daughter of his own, which clearly gave him some sort of mystical insight into the whole thing. Parenthood did that: turned perfectly intelligent, discerning adults into misty-eyed fools.

Even his own brother—the eminently rational Rico—hadn't been entirely immune, he thought with a stab of anguish. From the moment Luciana had been born her every yawn, every smile, had been scrutinized and analysed with an intense interest to which Luis had found it impossible to relate.

And still did.

Guilt lashed through him—familiar, but still painful enough to make him tense and catch his breath. Tomás threw him a curious glance and Luis forced a smile, keeping his eyes fixed straight ahead while the blurry impression of Luciana's small face swam into his mind's eye.

He couldn't even remember with any sort of clarity what she looked like. Or when he'd last seen her. How old was she now?

Another whiplash of guilt struck him as he realised he didn't know for sure. Five, was it? Or six? It had been ten months since Rico and Christiana had died, and Luciana had been five at the time—he knew that because the newspapers had focused so relentlessly on the tragedy of being orphaned at such a young age. Luis's hands were curled into fists. Had she had a birthday since then?

The performance on the stage appeared to have ended, and the children curtsied with varying degrees of grace. Automatically Luis joined in the applause, taking advantage of the opportunity to lean over and say quietly to Tomás, 'It is finished?'

'Not quite, sir. I believe there's one more item on the programme. Are you all right?'

'Never better,' Luis murmured blandly.

Part of the punishment was bearing the pain alone, in silence. He didn't have the right to share its burden.

He settled uncomfortably back as a line of little girls in snowy white tutus filed onto the stage. These ones were younger than the last group, smaller and more intimidated by the presence of the audience. A collective 'ahhh' went up from the rows of people behind Luis as they shuffled into position, sucking their fingers and looking out beyond the stage lights with huge, solemn eyes.

The music began—*Dance of the Little Swans*. Luis wasn't sure whether to laugh at the clichéd predictibility of it, or weep for the protracted torment. Instead he arranged his face into what he hoped was an expression of appreciation and watched as the children raised their arms and began to bend their knees in a series of careful pliés.

One little girl at the back stood still, frozen in anguish. The other children rose up onto their tiptoes and pirouetted shakily, but the only movement she made was that of her wide, terrified eyes which kept darting to the safety of the wings. The girl next to her was unimpressed by her failure to perform and nudged her heartily in the ribs.

Laughter rippled through the audience. At the front of the stage the other children were stolidly going through their routine, pointing toes, making sweeping movements of their arms and casting occasional furious glances at their classmate at the back. Luis watched her. Maybe it was because he'd just been thinking about his little niece, but something about the girl onstage reminded him of Luciana, even though she looked nothing like her. No doubt a psychiatrist would enjoy explaining that it was just another manifestation of guilt. The child before him had shrunk backwards a little so she was standing outside the spotlight's glare, but other than that she hadn't moved, and from his place of honour in the front row he could see the glisten of tears in her eyes and the tremble of her bottom lip.

And then it struck him. It wasn't just his tormented mind playing tricks on him; it was her attitude of patient suffering, of dignified misery, that reminded him of Luciana. He had seen the same expression on the face of his little niece, sensed the same silent anguish in her in the little time he'd spent with her, and it had made him feel every bit as helpless as he did now.

It wasn't a good feeling.

A movement in the wings caught his eye. Keeping to the shadows, an older girl ran lightly across the back of the stage and dropped to her knees beside her. For a moment Luis was too relieved to register properly the narrow, very straight back, the glossy dark plait that hung heavily between her shoulder blades, but then she stood again and it was impossible not to notice the length of her extremely shapely legs encased in thick black tights.

She was wearing a short black skirt and a fitted T-shirt, emblazoned across the back of which were the words *Pink Flamingo*.

Ten months ago he had made a vow to his brother and buried his appetite for women and excess alongside Rico in the family vault on Santosa. Now Luis felt his dormant interest flicker almost painfully back to life. Leaning over to Tomás he whispered, 'Isn't the Pink Flamingo a gentlemen's club?'

'I wouldn't know, sir.'

No, of course not. But Luis did, and he was intrigued to know what a girl who worked in a lap-dancing club was doing helping out at a children's ballet show. Bending down, still with her back to the audience, the Pink Flamingo girl took the little dancer's hand and whispered something in her ear. Relief spread across the small, pinched face as the older girl turned around and began to join in the steps of the dance.

Deus, she was stunning. Towering above the tiny children on the stage she looked every bit the haughty, graceful swan amongst a gaggle of fluffy, ungainly cygnets. Beside her the little girl who had looked so lost a moment ago was now smiling tremulously, growing in confidence and stature by the second.

He watched the precise movements of her slender legs, the upright set of her shoulders and head, and felt a prickle of unease at the back of his neck. Dragging his gaze upwards to her face he blinked, frowning suddenly and leaning forwards in astonishment and disbelief.

It was incredible… impossible…

It was Emily Balfour.

CHAPTER TWO

'EMILY—are you in there?'

Kiki's voice echoed off the tiles in the gloomy ladies' loo. Slumped against the door of the middle cubicle, Emily gritted her teeth to disguise their chattering and tried to sound normal as she answered.

'Yes, I'm here. Won't be a second.'

'Well, make sure you're not. You just got yourself a royal audience, honey. The prince is coming backstage and he's specifically asked to meet you so you'd better get out here quick.'

Emily opened the door and looked at Kiki with huge, anguished eyes. 'I can't, Kiki. Really—I mean, I'm hardly dressed for meeting royalty and I've only worked here for a couple of months anyway so—'

'Hey.' Kiki's kind face was creased with concern. 'Forget about what you're wearing. What's wrong, baby? You look dreadful.'

A quick glance at her reflection in the mirror above the sink told Emily that Kiki was absolutely right. Her face, always pale, was now the eerie white of an extra in a vampire movie, a fact which was emphasized by the way her dark hair was held severely back in her plait. She attempted a wan smile. 'Thanks. I'm fine. It was just being on stage… dancing in front of an audience, with the music and everything, and—'

Kiki made a sympathetic noise. 'Nerves, eh?'

No, Emily was going to say. Not nerves. More an absence

of nerves. An absence of anything. She was just going through the motions as if she'd been programmed—*why couldn't she feel it any more?*

'Anyway,' Kiki continued a little breathlessly before she had a chance to speak, 'the Prince was very impressed. He wants to meet you, and your dance group. I've got them all lined up on the stage, and they're really excited so hurry up.'

'OK, I'm coming.' Emily ran her hands under the tap and splashed cold water on her face to try to bring some colour to her cheeks. 'Which prince is it anyway?' she said into the depths of the basin.

But it was too late. Kiki had already gone, and the only answer was the bang of the door behind her. Left alone, Emily stared at her reflection in the mirror, not seeing her pinched face but looking instead into the bleakness of a future without dancing. God, less than a year ago when she'd danced the part of Sleeping Beauty in the Royal Ballet School's final production, no one would have been surprised at the idea of her meeting royalty backstage after a performance. But as a soloist at Covent Garden, not in the capacity of an unpaid teacher in a struggling community arts centre.

But that had been when she could dance. In the few brief, brilliant months when the technical skill she'd built over all those years of training had come together with something else—the indefinable, dangerous *something* Luis Cordoba had unlocked in her when his beautiful mouth had covered hers in the darkness beneath the trees.

She let out a long breath, turning away from the mirror and smoothing her T-shirt down. A lot had happened in a year.

She pulled open the door and went back to join the children. She'd kicked her shoes off when she went onto the stage and the rough parquet floor snagged at her tights as she hurried back along the corridor. Great, she thought despairingly. That was all she needed. She was so behind with the rent on her horrible bedsit that buying a loaf of bread felt like wanton extravagance at the moment. Tights were as beyond her budget these days as a designer ball gown.

She ran lightly up the steps to the back of the stage. Beyond the wings she could see her class of little dancers lined up and standing very straight, which, along with the deep rumble of male voices, told her that the royal party was already there. Ducking her head she slipped silently onto the stage and took her place at the end of the line, glancing along the row of children as she did so.

Emily's heart stopped.

His head was bent as he talked to one of the little girls, the stage lights shining on his broad, perfectly muscled shoulders and picking out the gold strands in his deliciously untidy tawny hair. Her stomach dissolved with horror. Oh, God. It was him. It was really him. The royalty Kiki had been talking about was Luis Cordoba, Crown Prince of Santosa, and he was making his way quickly along the line towards her.

Too quickly. The little dancers bobbed curtsies as he passed them, but he barely glanced at them. Emily had the sensation of standing on the track in the path of a speeding train, knowing that the moment of impact was almost upon her. He wouldn't recognize her, she reassured herself desperately. Why would he? They'd only met once—and then only for a couple of minutes in a situation which was a world away from this. He must meet thousands of women…*kiss thousands of women*….

Someone was speaking. Dimly, Emily registered that it was one of the council members who'd been round to look at the Larchfield premises in expectation of the youth centre's closure. 'This is one of the valuable volunteers who bring new experiences into the lives of our young people. Miss Jones is a graduate of the Royal Ballet School….'

Like an automaton Emily bent her head and sank down in a curtsy. From an etiquette point of view it was the right thing to do, but more importantly it also gave her a great chance to avoid looking up at the man she'd last seen in the garden at Balfour, when he'd drawn her into the shadow of the trees and kissed her with an arrogance and an expertise which shocked and thrilled and horrified her.

Call me when you grow up...

She steeled herself, and looked up.

The express train hit. For a moment the breath was knocked out of her and it was like falling. Like skydiving into the sunset. And then realizing that you didn't have a parachute.

Luis Cordoba raised one fine eyebrow a fraction. Beneath it his eyes were a hard, dull gold. 'Really, Miss *Jones*?'

Oh, God. That sexy accent. Not Spanish—Kiki had been wrong about that. Portuguese. It almost distracted her from the slight emphasis he placed on her name. Or—correction—the random name she'd given when she started volunteering at Larchfield. There was a part of her that had hated the deception and felt that she was betraying the friends she had made by keeping her real identity secret, but the anonymity was like armour. It was her protection and she'd clung to it. And now she felt like she was standing there, naked and wrapped only in the skimpiest of towels, and that the man standing in front of her had hold of the corner and was ready to pull it off her. Just for fun.

'Y-yes,' she stammered, looking up into that lean and perfect face, silently begging him not to give her away.

'The Royal Ballet?' he said softly. 'And from there you've chosen to come here to teach these children instead of concentrating on your own dancing career? Impressively altruistic. Your family must be very proud of you.'

Only she could hear the hint of challenge in his low, velvety voice. So he did recognize her, and he clearly knew exactly where to insert the knife, how to inflict the deepest wound where it wouldn't show. She could feel the eyes of everyone in the room—the council officials, Kiki, the children getting restless now—on her, but all of them combined were nothing compared to his cool, metallic glare.

'I'd like to think they would be,' she said breathlessly, and instantly regretted it. The words *if they knew* hung in the air between them, and she waited for him to say them out loud. But Luis Cordoba didn't play things the straightforward way.

He nodded, slowly, and for a long moment his eyes stayed locked with hers. And then his gaze flickered downwards to the Pink Flamingo logo on the front of her black T-shirt.

'It's good to know that you haven't given up dancing altogether though,' he said gravely. A brief smile pulled at the corners of his mouth. 'Keep up the good work, Miss—?'

'Jones,' she croaked.

And then he was being ushered forwards by the council officials, who were no doubt keen to take him outside and show him the all-weather football pitch, a fraction of which had been paid for by a council grant. Out of the arc-light beam of his gaze Emily felt like a puppet that had suddenly had its strings cut. Around her the children relaxed into excited chatter, relieved at being released from the need to be on their best behaviour. Emily felt numb.

He'd got it all wrong. Bloody T-shirt. She wanted to run after him and grab his arm, force him to turn round so she could explain that she didn't dance at the Pink Flamingo—she worked behind the bar. He might have awoken something in her when he'd kissed her, but he hadn't changed her whole personality for God's sake….

But he was gone, leaving nothing but a whisper of his masculine, expensive scent in the air. The lights seemed to dim and the shadows around her thicken. It was too late.

The wolf had slipped back into the forest, and she was safe.

So why didn't she feel more relieved?

'Stop the car.'

Tomás looked round sharply, surprised. 'Sir?'

Luis stared straight ahead, his fingers drumming on the walnut inlay of the door. 'We'll wait here for a while, and then we'll go back.'

'Back, sir?' Tomás looked alarmed. 'Why? I thought you'd
be keen to leave here as quickly as possible.'

'I was. I am. But not without bringing "Miss Jones" with me.'

Alarm had turned to a mixture of panic and horror on
Tomás's open face now. 'Sir…if I may say so, that's not a good
idea. The press office… The papers… The purpose of this trip
was to put all those stories firmly in the past.'

'They *are* firmly in the past,' Luis said with quiet, emphatic
bitterness. 'When was the last time I picked up a girl for a one-
night stand?'

'The public have long memories, sir. And those photos of
you falling out of nightclubs and groping women in the back
of the car still get published regularly. If the newspapers get
hold of this…this Miss Jones…'

Luis smiled. 'You mean if she were to kiss and tell?'

'Exactly, sir. She could profit handsomely from such a story.'

'My night of passion with the playboy prince?' Luis suggested mockingly, then shook his head. 'She wouldn't do that.'

'With respect, sir, you don't know that for sure. Some of
these girls have no concept of privacy…'

'With respect, Tomás, I do know it for sure, because I also
know that that girl has considerably more to hide than I do. I'm
not going to seduce her—I'm going to find out what a nice girl
like Emily Balfour is doing in a place like this.'

'Emily *Balfour*, sir? But I thought her name was—'

'Jones? No. That, Tomás, was Oscar's youngest daughter.
Or the one that used to be his youngest until a subsequent
claimant to the position arrived on the doorstep.' Looking out
of the window Luis frowned slightly.

'I'll ask security to go in and get her, shall I, sir?' Tomás
asked, glancing nervously around. 'This probably isn't the best
place to hang around.'

'The car is fully bullet-proof,' Luis reminded him drily.
'We're quite safe. And I don't think she'll respond well to
being hauled out by security. As I recall from last year, Emily

Balfour won't be pushed into doing anything she doesn't want to.'

'Ah, here she is now, sir,' Tomás said with evident relief. 'I'll just get—'

But Luis had already got out of the car. Tomás swore with uncharacteristic crudeness, whipping his mobile phone out of his pocket and speed-dialling the head of security in the other car. At times he found the Crown Prince's lack of regard for protocol and formality refreshing, but mostly it was just a giant pain in the backside. He just hadn't seemed to grasp that, since his brother and sister-in-law's shocking deaths, he was the future of Santosa.

God help them.

Trying to prepare Luis to take the reins of his ailing father was like taking a tiger from the jungle and trying to teach it to jump through hoops. Difficult and dangerous. And, he thought gloomily, if anything went wrong he would be the one to get his head bitten off.

''Night, Kiki—see you tomorrow!'

Hastily, not waiting for a reply, Emily slipped out of the door and into the cool, blue evening, wrapping her cardigan tightly around her. Usually she waited while Kiki locked up and the two of them walked part of the way home together, but tonight she just wanted to get out of there and be alone.

'Can I offer you a lift?'

She jumped, giving a little gasp of shock as a figure emerged from the twilight and stood in front of her, barring her way.

'Sorry,' said the same husky, amused drawl. 'I didn't mean to startle you. But I think that just proves my point that it's really not safe for you to be out on the streets on your own in the dark. It's just as well I'm not some drug-crazed youth with a gun in his hand.'

'I'll take my chances, thank you,' Emily muttered, attempting to slip past him. But he was too quick for her. She bit back another gasp as strong fingers closed around her wrist, stopping her in her tracks and pulling her back round so she was facing him.

From the shadows beyond the car someone said something in rapid Portuguese. Luis didn't turn his head, didn't loosen his grip, didn't take his eyes from hers. '*Sim, obrigado*, Tomás.' he said curtly. 'This won't take long.'

'No, it won't,' she said shakily, 'because I'm not going anywhere with you. Goodbye…'

It was said with more hope than conviction. Her heart was hammering out an uneven rhythm against her ribs, her whole body flooded with adrenaline. In the violet dusk his face was indistinct, but she could see the shadows beneath his aristocratic cheekbones and the glitter of his eyes.

'What a disappointment. I saw that Pink Flamingo T-shirt and just assumed you'd grown up a bit since last time we met.'

'I have.' She spoke through gritted teeth. 'Which is why I'm not getting into a car with you. Now, if you'll let me go, it's been a long day and I want to get home.'

He let her go without resistance. 'Funny. That's what I wanted to talk to you about.'

The icy edge to his voice stopped her in her tracks and filled her with sudden misgiving. She turned back to him.

'What?'

'Home.' He paused, his face impossible to read in the gloom. Emily felt the hairs rise on the back of her neck. Beyond the black car that waited behind him she could hear the sound of voices from the street, the distant wail of a siren. 'I was at Balfour Manor last night.'

A door slammed inside the community centre. Emily darted an anxious glance over her shoulder, hoping Kiki hadn't heard him. 'Please…' she implored.

In one smooth movement he turned and pulled open the car door. 'Perhaps you'd prefer to have this conversation in the car, before your cover is blown and your new friends find out that "Miss Jones" is really the daughter of a billionaire who could end all the financial problems of this extremely valuable community resource just by asking Daddy nicely....'

Emily shrank back, as if the plush interior of the car was the mouth of a giant whale, waiting to swallow her up. Her voice was cracked and faint. 'But I have nothing to say to you.'

'That's fine.' His voice was cool as he placed a hand in the small of her back and brought her forward. 'You can just listen.'

There was someone else in the car—a man in his thirties perhaps, in a dark suit. He smiled as Emily slid reluctantly onto the seat beside him, and she felt slightly reassured. At least she wouldn't be alone with Luis.

On the downside, there wasn't so much room. As Luis finished speaking to the driver and got in beside her, Emily found herself far closer than was comfortable to his long, hard thigh on the seat. The only alternative was to move more towards the silent, suited man on her other side. Forget 'better the devil you know,' she thought miserably. No one could be more dangerous than Luis Cordoba. She inched away, hoping he wouldn't notice.

No such luck.

'That's Tomás, my private secretary,' Luis said sardonically. 'You can sit on his knee, if you like. He's very good with children.'

Tomás smiled, with the indulgent air of someone who had seen all this before. 'Take no notice of His Highness, Miss Balfour.'

'Thank you, Tomás.' Emily turned back to Luis. 'I'm not a child, and you're certainly not my father, so I don't know why you think you can order me around.'

The car pulled out of the Larchfield compound and onto the road. 'Thank goodness I'm not your father,' Luis said laconically. 'From what I saw of him yesterday Oscar isn't a happy man.'

'W-what do you mean?'

'Well, there's all this for a start.' He leaned forward and plucked a copy of the newspaper Emily had bought earlier from a pocket in the back of the driver's seat.

Holding her head up very stiffly she glanced at it in distaste. 'I know. I've seen it. Look, don't you want to know where I live?'

'No, not really,' he said in a bored voice. 'Not unless you're going to insist on going back there to change.'

A dart of alarm shot through her. 'Change? Into what?'

'Anything that wasn't hand knitted by medieval peasants from yak's wool,' he suggested disdainfully, his gaze travelling downwards from her cardigan to the cheap, flat shoes she'd bought for work. 'As disguises go I must say you've chosen very well. Who would have thought one of the celebrated Balfour girls would go around dressed like a refugee from a hippy commune?'

Emily raised her chin, ignoring the jibe. 'Why would I want to change? Where are we going?' A horrible thought occurred to her. 'Not home? Not back to Balfour, because I can't. I—'

'Relax.' He cut through her mounting panic. 'I'm taking you out to dinner.'

'Isn't it polite to ask first?' Emily slumped back against the seat, folding her arms mutinously. Of course, the normal rules of courtesy didn't apply to the Prince of Santosa. His title made him think he could do anything and have anything. Or anyone.

'If I had asked would you have accepted?' he said evenly.

She shook her head.

'Exactly. Just think of it as being cruel to be kind.'

Emily gave a bark of harsh laughter. 'The cruelty I can believe. Kindness? Not so much.'

'When was the last time you ate properly?

Emily thought back to the bowl of cut-price breakfast cereal she'd had in her room before leaving for work earlier. The milk had been off, so she hadn't felt like eating much. The rent she paid for her room in Mr Lukacs's house was supposed to include use of the kitchen, but she found that whenever she ventured in there he would appear, finding some excuse to squeeze past her in the narrow space, or just watching her with his damp, beady eyes. She preferred to avoid it.

'Why do you care? It's got nothing to do with you.'

Despair made her uncharacteristically ungracious. Despair

and the uncomfortable feeling that, having been hit by the express train, she had now been hauled aboard and was speeding away into unknown and dangerous territory.

'You're right, it's not. Not in itself, and believe me I have plenty of other things to worry about. But given that your father looks like a dead man walking because he has no idea where you are, and I discover you living like…like…' Lost for words, he gave a small exhalation of frustration. 'It's become my business whether I like it or not. So I'm going to feed you, and you're going to tell me exactly what's going on.'

Something in his tone silenced the retort that had sprung to her lips. There was an edge there, a tension that she hadn't noticed in him before. The Luis Cordoba she knew was laughing, insouciant, urbane—a playboy whose most serious decisions in life involved which party invitations to accept, and which women to seduce when he got there.

This man was different. Harder. Colder. And possibly even more dangerous than before.

The car had picked up speed now. The street lights stained the soft, early summer dusk a lurid shade of orange, and threw neon bars of light into the car as they sped along. They were heading out of the city, she realised with curious numbness. When he had said dinner she had imagined some exclusive West End restaurant, but the traffic was thinning as they left London behind them.

The events of the exhausting day seemed to pile up in the centre of Emily's mind, blocking her ability to think properly. Instead she sat motionless between the dark-suited men, keeping herself very upright, her eyes fixed straight ahead of her.

A dead man walking.

The phrase echoed in her head. She longed to ask Luis what he meant, what Oscar had said, but couldn't bring herself to do it in the presence of Tomás and the faceless driver. The damned newspaper still lay on the seat between them, its salacious headline seeming to emit some high-frequency signal into her brain, which made it impossible to quite ignore it. Her chest felt like there was an iron band across it as she thought of Zoe, and Olivia and Bella—what were they doing now, in the aftermath of the latest shocking news? And her father…

Suddenly she felt very tired, and knew that it wasn't just from the events of the day. It was from the past two months of fighting to keep her head above water since she'd left home—of battling loneliness, the grimness of her surroundings, the shock of struggling to make ends meet for the first time in her life. It was from before that too—from the sheer, grinding misery of missing her mother, mourning her death and her father's betrayal.

She tipped her head back against the cushioning leather and closed her eyes. In the darkness behind their lids she was even more aware of Luis beside her. He was lounging nonchalantly, but she could sense the restlessness that lurked beneath his outward show of calm, the strength and steely determination that infused his whole being.

And as her head drooped onto his shoulder and the soapy sweet scent of hawthorn drifted in on the warm May evening she forgot to be afraid of him.

She felt simply…safe.

CHAPTER THREE

'OSCAR, it's Luis.'

At the other end of the line there was a slight pause. 'Luis—how good of you to phone.' The words were polite enough, but couldn't quite disguise the weariness and disappointment in Oscar Balfour's voice. 'If it was just to say thank-you for last night's party, I can assure you, there was no need.'

'You credit me with rather more courtesy than I have, I'm afraid.' Luis smiled, playing idly with the silken fringe on the overstuffed cushion beside him. 'I wasn't ringing to thank you, but to let you know that I've found Emily.'

'*Emily?*' Instantly Oscar was alert, and the rawness of the emotion in his voice almost made Luis flinch. 'My God, Luis—where? Is she all right?'

'Yes.' He paused for a fraction of a second, thinking of the sharpness of her cheekbones, her bird-like fragility, the shadows beneath her eyes. 'She's fine. She's teaching ballet to some inner-city kids in one of the charity projects I visited today.' He thought it better not to mention the Pink Flamingo.

'In town? Tell me where. I'll get Fleming to bring the car and get there as soon as I can.'

'No point.' Getting up, Luis sloshed some whisky into a glass. 'I've brought her down to my hotel for dinner. From what I gather in the papers you have enough on your plate today already. Let me talk to her, and I'll update you tomorrow.'

Oscar hesitated, and when he spoke again he sounded old and uncertain—a million miles from the elegant patriarch of one of Britain's most celebrated families, the powerful businessman at the helm of a billion-dollar empire. 'All right. As you say, I have a few things to sort out here. You'll probably handle her a lot better than I can anyway.' He sighed heavily. 'We had an argument, when Mia arrived, and afterwards she completely cut herself off from me. That's what kills me, Luis—she just wouldn't talk to me at all. I didn't push it. Lillian was dying—'

His voice cracked, and Luis took a large swig of whisky while he waited for him to continue. 'Nothing else seemed important. I thought that afterwards… when Lillian was gone I'd have time to talk to Emily, explain about Mia. But I didn't get the chance. She left the day after the funeral.'

'Did she give you any clue that she was going?'

Oscar gave a ragged, humourless laugh. 'That was the hardest thing of all. Her leaving was so complete and so unexpected. No drama, no big scene. She just…*did it*—severed all her ties with us completely. She didn't take anything with her—only her ballet things and the clothes she was wearing. She even left her mobile phone, which was a very obvious way of letting me know she didn't want any further contact.'

Luis frowned. 'She was serious about not being found, then.'

'Oh, yes. But that's Emily. She doesn't do anything in half-measures. Never has. Whatever she does she does passionately, with her whole heart and soul. I've always admired her for that—I suppose it's what made her do so well at dancing—but the trouble is she applies the same rigorous standards that she expects from herself to those around her. I've let her down—it's as simple as that. She thought I was decent and honourable, and now she's found out that I'm not.'

Luis let his eyelids flicker closed for a second. 'None of us are,' he said savagely.

'Lillian was,' Oscar said simply, 'and Emily is so like her.

She's good, through and through. But strong too. She'd do anything for the people she loves.'

The memory of the little girl on stage earlier came back to Luis—the way Emily had taken her hand and danced alongside her, giving her the courage to carry on.

'I'm sorry.' Oscar's rueful voice broke into his thoughts. 'I'm boring you to death. Look, Luis, I'm so relieved that you've found her and that she's all right. That's the main thing, but if you could…'

The sentence trailed off. 'Yes?' Luis prompted. 'What would you like me to do?'

Oscar laughed despairingly. 'I was going to say, if you could make her understand…but of course that's unreasonable.'

Meditatively, Luis swirled the dark amber liquid round in his glass and then drained it in one mouthful. 'We'll see, Oscar. Leave it with me. I'll see what I can do.'

'Thank you, Luis. I'm grateful.'

'My pleasure.'

'You'll be all right here, Miss Balfour?'

Standing blinking in the doorway, Emily looked around the opulent room in front of her, and then turned to look at Tomás in alarm. 'I—I don't understand… whose room is this?'

'Yours, Miss.' Tomás's tone was soothing. 'Since you're so tired His Highness thought you might like a chance to freshen up before dinner. Maybe to have a bath and relax a little before eating?'

Emily regarded the elegant antique furnishings, the soft lighting, the vases of flowers, warily, wondering what the catch was.

'Where is Lu—His Highness?'

'The Prince has a suite on the floor above, Miss Balfour. He's in there right now having a drink and making some phone calls. Would you like me to ask him to come down when he's finished?'

'Oh, no, thank you,' Emily said hastily. 'No, it's fine. I'd love to have a bath.'

If only to put off the moment when she'd have to face Luis Cordoba over the dinner table, she thought, stepping forward and feeling her feet sink into the thick pile of the cream carpet. The room was huge, decorated in a classic English country house style which—apart from the addition of a Victorian-style bath standing on a raised platform in front of the huge French windows—was poignantly reminiscent of Lillian's pretty bedroom at Balfour. Or at least how it had been before the paraphernalia of illness had crept in to spoil its carefully designed scheme.

'Very good, Miss Balfour. Perhaps you could phone down to reception when you're ready? One of our staff will be there to accept the message.' Tomás left, quietly shutting the door behind him, and Emily wandered slowly over to the dressing table, running her fingers along its polished surface as if in a dream.

She leaned forward, looking into the mirror, where her own eyes stared back at her—smudged and dark with exhaustion. She was so tired, maybe it *was* a dream. Maybe she'd wake up any minute and find herself back in the narrow, lumpy bed in her bedsit, beneath sheets from which no amount of trips to the launderette could remove the smell of damp….

But then she remembered Luis Cordoba was waiting for her and felt her stomach clench with painful unease that left her in no doubt that she was wide awake. Compared to where she'd just come from this place might look and feel like paradise, but it certainly wasn't without its serpents.

She straightened up quickly, tugging the band from the end of her plait and loosening her hair with shaking fingers.

She'd been stupid to let her guard down by falling asleep in the car, but just for a moment it had felt so wonderful not to have to think any more. She was so tired of thinking, and the relief of having someone come along and take over, tell her what was going to happen and what she had to do, was profound.

It's just a shame that that someone was a shallow, untrustworthy playboy whose interest in women extended only as far as the bedroom, she thought, crossing the room to where the bath stood in decadent splendour. Although today he hadn't actually shown so much as a flicker of interest in her, she reflected miserably as she turned on the taps and remembered the cool, dismissive way he'd looked her over.

She stripped off quickly, wincing as she pricked her finger on the safety pin that held up the black skirt she'd bought in a charity shop. She threw it onto the bed, where it looked more depressingly cheap and nasty than ever against the silk coverlet and the smooth Egyptian cotton sheets. Quickly she reached for the hotel bathrobe that was folded, fat as a cushion, on the end of the bed and put it on, wrapping its miraculous softness around her too-thin body.

She could hardly blame him for not being interested in her.

Even she was repelled by the jut of her hipbones, the hard ridges of her ribs beneath her skin, so she had no illusions about anyone else feeling differently. Especially not a connoisseur of the female form like Luis Cordoba. *Call me when you grow up,* he'd taunted. But she hadn't just grown up in the past year. She'd grown *old*.

The bath was full. Turning the taps off Emily shrugged off the bathrobe and hastily slipped into the water, lying back so that it covered her body completely. Closing her eyes she inhaled deeply, savouring the exotic, expensive fragrance of the designer bath oil and trying to refocus her thoughts. It was criminal to let anything spoil this moment of rare luxury. Sinking farther down in the deep water she exhaled again, feeling some of the tension that had taken up permanent residence in her shoulders lately ebb away, and with it a little of her iron-hard resolve.

God, she missed the physical comforts of her old life at Balfour. The day after Lillian's funeral, when she'd walked out with nothing but a heart full of hurt and a head full of moral indignation, if she had known what she was letting herself in for she might have hesitated for a second before slamming that imposing door behind her. Her leaving was hardly planned, it was simply a logical response to what she'd come to consider an intolerable situation. She needed time and space to come to terms with what had happened, and she'd imagined going to London, getting a place in one of the major ballet companies there, and finding herself a pleasant, sunny flat in an area where popping out to buy a pint of milk wasn't an extreme sport....

In other words, behaving like a grown-up.

How naive she'd been. Sheltered from reality by the Balfour wealth, she hadn't even known how much a pint of milk cost.

She had easily got auditions with three ballet companies, but it seemed that the months of grief and turmoil had taken their toll in ways she couldn't have begun to anticipate. Each audition passed in an excruciating embarrassment of clumsy footwork, mechanical arm movements and missed timing. It was as if she had lead weights inside her, pulling her down. As if she was trying to dance with a heart full of cement.

She had failed to win a place with any company.

After that nothing seemed to matter much. She had lost everything she cared about, and it simply became a matter of survival, which meant finding somewhere to live and a means of income. The advertisement for the job at the Pink Flamingo had caught her eye because it contained the word *dancing*.

It was only as she'd stepped into the beer-and-nicotine-scented gloom when she'd gone to see about the job that she realised what kind of dancing it was. Horrified, she had told the oily man into whose seedy office she was shown that she had made a mistake, but after running his eyes shrewdly over her he had offered her a job behind the bar.

Realising she had no choice but to accept it had been one of the lowest points of her life.

But she wasn't going to think about that now. She had survived the past two months by using the self-discipline she had acquired during her years at ballet school to block out the bad stuff and focus on small pleasures and triumphs: sharing a coffee with Kiki in Larchfield's shabby kitchen, seeing the pride on the faces of the little girls in her ballet class when they learned a new position. And now this…relaxing in a warm, scented bath as the twilight deepened beyond the windows and the scent of gardenia filled her senses. This was bliss. Heaven. In fact the pleasure of the moment was so exquisite that it almost made the past two miserable months worth it, just to feel this good.

She breathed in again, lifting her feet out of the water and resting them on the edge of the bath, flexing her toes and feeling the taut muscles in her insteps soften. The only sound was the trickling of the water, and the soft sigh of her own breathing, and she suddenly realised how much she'd missed silence. At Balfour she had taken that—like so much else—completely for granted. She simply hadn't realised what a luxury it was to lie in bed and not be kept awake by cars revving their engines in the street below, by people shouting and the noises of fights and drunken laughter.

She closed her eyes, steadying the rhythm of her breathing, emptying her mind and consciously relaxing her body. Her chin sank beneath the water as the tension ebbed from her neck. She should probably get out, she thought distantly, but it felt too good just to lie there. She inhaled, exhaled, slipping farther down in the water, losing herself in the swirling darkness behind her closed eyes as warmth and peace enveloped her, and she finally felt safe enough to let go….

She came to the second her nose touched the water. Instinctively sucking in a breath she was suddenly choking on water, gasping and spluttering as her lungs filled, flailing wildly as she struggled to raise herself upright.

Someone was holding her, lifting her high out of the water. Angels? She waited for the moment when she would look down and see herself lying there in the bath, but her body felt all too present as she felt the iron-hard chest she was being held against, and the tawny tiger's eyes that were looking down into her face were a far cry from angelic.

She wasn't dead, then.

It was much worse than that.

She was lying in Luis Cordoba's arms, and she was stark naked.

She wasn't dead.

Seeing her like that—so still, her hair floating around her face like seaweed, and not a breath or a ripple disturbing the mirror-flat surface of the water—he had felt a moment of panic, along with the painful stirring of memories long buried.

Dropping her slippery, glistening body unceremoniously onto the bed he turned to pick up the bathrobe she'd dropped on the floor beside the bath.

'Here. Put this on,' he drawled acidly. 'There's little point in bothering to save you from drowning if you then catch your death of cold.'

Still coughing, she sat up, bringing her long legs up to her chest and wrapping her arms tightly around them. Grabbing the bathrobe from him she clutched it against her. 'Don't look,' she croaked, 'Please…'

With elaborate courtesy Luis turned and walked over to the large windows, staring out into the blue dusk, his heart still beating sickeningly hard. 'Considering you work in a lap-dancing club, isn't the modesty a bit misplaced?'

'I don't dance there—I work behind the bar,' she said through chattering teeth. And then she added almost in an undertone, 'I don't dance anywhere any more.'

'Can I turn round now?' Why did he feel relieved?

'Yes.'

She was sitting huddled up against the bed's plump, padded headboard. Her damp hair was pushed back from her face, emphasising the sharpness of her cheekbones and the shadows beneath her eyes. Eyes that were looking at him as if she were expecting him to tie her up and ravish her at knifepoint.

'I'm sure I wouldn't have drowned,' she said miserably. 'I would definitely have woken up when—'

Luis cut her off with a sharp, impatient sound. 'Forgive me for not testing that theory. Next time I'll wait until you've been under the water for a few minutes before I haul you out.'

And have one more life on his conscience.

'There won't be a *next time*.' She drew the robe more tightly around her, pulled her knees more closely to her body, her eyes sapphire pools of anguish. 'There shouldn't have been a *this time*. What were you doing watching me in the bath?'

'You didn't answer when I knocked, so I came in,' he said coldly. 'I half expected to find you'd escaped through the French windows and bolted into the night, but I wasn't prepared for a suicide bid.'

'It was not—' she retorted hotly, and was about to argue more when there was a knock on the door.

'That'll be dinner,'

'*Dinner?* But—'

She sprang to her feet as two pretty room-service staff brought in cumbersome trolleys laden with silver-domed dishes and, with much blushing and fluttering of eyelashes, asked Luis where he'd like them. He ignored the obvious double entendre that would have sprung from his lips without a second thought in his old life. '*Obrigado*. Just leave them there,' he said, with the briefest of smiles before turning back to Emily. 'You seemed too tired to want to go down to the restaurant. I thought you'd prefer to eat up here. Is that OK?'

Emily tried not to let the shock that ricocheted through her show on her face. She waited until the door had closed behind the pretty waitresses before turning to him, unable to keep the outrage from her voice. 'No, it's not OK! It's impossible. I bet they think that we're…' She could feel a tide of colour wash into her cheeks. 'That we've…'

Utterly unmoved by her discomfort Luis was already uncovering dishes and pouring wine. 'Just had sex?' he suggested.

'Exactly!'

'Frankly, *querida*, I doubt it.' Coming towards the bed with a plate of smoked-salmon sandwiches and two glasses of wine Luis smiled lazily, but his eyes were cold. 'If we had you wouldn't be so bad tempered. Now, come and eat.'

She watched in alarm as he swung his long legs onto the bed and leaned back against the pile of pillows. 'B-but I'm not dressed,' she stammered.

'Believe me, you look a lot more respectable like that than in that awful cardigan.'

She took a deep breath, determined to rise above his taunting. 'Look, I didn't ask for any of this. I don't want—'

But Luis cut her off, his voice suddenly edged with steel. 'The thing is, *amada*, right now I'm not overly bothered about what *you* want. This isn't just about you, I'm afraid. It's about your family. Your father. He's just lost his wife—do you really think now was a good time for him to cope with losing a daughter too?'

Emily gave a short, bitter laugh. 'I think it was the perfect time, since he'd just gained another one to take my place.'

Luis speared her with his gold-flecked eyes and nodded slowly. 'I thought as much. This is about Mia, isn't it?'

'No. No, it's not about Mia at all,' Emily said despairingly, sinking down onto the bed, as far away from him as possible, and taking a huge mouthful of wine. As its heat stole down inside her she could feel her defences slipping, melting away like snow in the glare of the sun. After two months of bottling it all up the urge to talk was suddenly overwhelming. 'I have nothing against Mia herself—she seems very sweet. It's hardly her fault.'

'What's not her fault?'

Pain knotted in Emily's throat, making it difficult to swallow the mouthful of smoked-salmon sandwich. 'That my father— sorry, *our* father—' she corrected, her voice dripping with irony '—was so weak and stupid that he had a meaningless one-night stand with a woman he'd never met the night before his wedding and got her pregnant.'

She waited. Waited for his expression of surprise at this revelation about Oscar Balfour—irreproachable pillar of the establishment.

It didn't come.

'No,' he agreed nonchalantly, taking another sandwich and devouring it in one bite. 'Accidents happen. You certainly couldn't blame Mia for the circumstances of her own conception. Anyway, what does it matter now? Oscar still married your mother and remained happily married to her for—what— twenty years?'

She frowned, staring down at the crust of bread between her fingers, crumbling it into tiny pieces. 'But it was based on lies,' she said in a choked voice. 'A good relationship can only be based on trust and truth. Love means not having secrets from someone, not having to hide anything.'

'Does it really?' he said softly, and with infinite scorn, as if what she had said was utterly facile. 'And what if there are things the other person would be better off not knowing?'

She lifted her head, forcing herself to look at him. 'Better for them, or better for you?'

He looked back at her. His eyes were narrowed, but for a fraction of a second she thought she saw something in them that was almost like uncertainty. 'Better for you both.'

'You have to trust the person enough to forgive you,' she said, emotion turning her voice husky. 'You have to give them a chance.'

He turned his head away from her and looked down. A lock of hair fell down over his eyes, making him look suddenly strangely unguarded. Emily felt a painful lurching sensation in her chest.

'And your father didn't do that?' he said tonelessly. 'He didn't tell her, even when Mia came?'

Emily shook her head, not wanting to remember those dark days after Mia had shown up. Days that slipped by like sand in a bottle. 'My father told us all to make sure she didn't suspect a thing.' She gave a bleak smile. 'Mia pretended to be the new housekeeper, which wasn't a great start to her life as a Balfour, but Mum had such little time left by then.'

Luis shrugged, leaning over to pick up the wine bottle from the bedside table. 'There you are, then. At least he spared her the pain of finding out.'

'What? So you think that makes it *OK*?' Angrily she snatched her glass away just as he was about to fill it, so that wine spilled onto her bare legs.

A muscle jumped beneath the bronzed skin of his cheek. The room suddenly seemed very still. 'I think it doesn't alter the fact that your parents had a good, happy marriage,' he said slowly.

Emily gave a snort of low, cynical laughter. 'Oh, right. Your definition of a happy marriage being one where you can screw around as often as you like and it doesn't matter as long as the other person doesn't find out? What a lucky woman the future Crown Princess of Santosa is.'

'That's different.' As if in slow motion she watched him reach out and catch the drip of wine that was running down her shin with his thumb. 'When I marry it'll be a business arrangement. Love will have no part in it, and I expect the future Crown Princess of Santosa will fully understand that.'

Emily turned to stone beneath his touch, terrified by the fire that was crackling along her nerves, like the fuse of a bomb. 'A business arrangement?' she rasped. 'The terms of which will make it perfectly OK for you to sleep with whoever you like. And will she be free to do the same?'

'As long as she's discreet,' he said softly, following the wet trail of the wine down her leg and over her ankle. 'Jealousy is a nasty disease to which, thankfully, I'm completely immune. I'm a realist. Marriage fulfils a lot of needs—in my case practical, in your father's case emotional. He loved Lillian, and one last fling before his wedding doesn't alter that. It meant nothing.'

'That's the bit I don't get,' Emily said, forcing her mind to stay focused on the subject, and not on the sparks of pleasure his touch had ignited beneath her skin. 'Why do it, then? Why have sex with someone if it means nothing?'

In the soft lamp light his face was beautiful but impossible to read. Thoughtfully he slid his hand beneath her instep, turning her foot round and studying it. Emily felt it flex helplessly, her toes curling downwards as if they had a life of their own. All the nerves of her body seemed suddenly to be concentrated in that foot, making it tingle as if with pins and needles. Distantly she remembered the sensation she used to get in her feet before a performance, how it felt as if they were coming alive.

'If you have to ask the question you probably wouldn't understand the answer,' Luis said dryly, his thumb massaging her high arch. 'Sexual attraction isn't something you can rationalize, or sometimes even control. It's called being human. Oscar might be your father but he's still just a human being.'

'I know that.' Her voice was quivering and breathless.

'And yet it seems to me that you want to punish him for it.' He ran his fingertips over the hard, shiny calluses at the base of her toes, adding softly, 'You have the most extraordinary feet.'

Sharply she pulled her foot from his grasp and stood, pacing over to the fireplace, desperate to get far enough away from him to think clearly—focus on the conversation they were having, not the very separate line of communication her body suddenly seemed intent on pursuing. 'It's not like that. I'm not punishing him. I just feel…betrayed. Everything feels like it's falling apart…with my mother and Mia and now Zoe and that…that… *stuff* in the paper today. It's like the whole family is damned or something—like some awful fairy tale where the wishes that the good fairy has given to the princesses turn out to be curses. The money and the good looks—they've just brought temptations that it seems no one can resist.'

'Except you.' He had got up and followed her to where she stood. Her back was towards him but in the mirror above the fireplace their eyes met and she felt her blood heat as he smiled right into them. 'As I recall, you resisted most forcefully last year.'

'Yes.' She wanted to look away, but she couldn't. 'Because I want more than that.'

He dropped his gaze, and she felt a split second of relief. But then he slid his hand beneath her hair and she stiffened again, gripped by emotions and sensations she couldn't identify or control. Or resist.

'Than what?' He said softly, gently stroking the back of her neck.

'Than quick…meaningless…sex.' She gasped.

'Don't knock it until you've tried it.' In contrast to her own voice, his was as smooth and slow and rich as sun-warmed honey.

'And what makes you think I haven't?'

It was a desperate attempt at bravado, but in the mirror she caught a brief glimpse of the golden gleam in his eyes as he bent his head and brushed his lips against her ear. Instinctively she flinched violently away from the thousand-watt electric shock that his touch sparked through her whole body.

He laughed softly. 'That.'

Trembling, breathing as heavily as if she'd just run a marathon, Emily faced him. Cheeks flaming, she pulled the collar of the robe up around her neck and raised her chin defiantly and attempted what she hoped was a scornful laugh. 'Just because I'm not willing to fall into bed with you the moment you click your fingers.'

Luis caught hold of the tie belt of the robe and pulled her gently towards him. 'I see,' he said gravely, wickedness glittering in the depths of his eyes, 'you expect foreplay too, do you? Something like this…'

She opened her mouth to protest, but before she could make the words come out his lips had covered hers and darkness had exploded inside her head, obliterating everything but him: the heat and closeness of his body, the scent and taste of him.

She was shocked rigid, shocked into helplessness, unable to think, to respond sensibly. She should be pulling away, but all she seemed to be capable of was standing as still and stiff as Joan of Arc at the stake with the flames licking up around her….

Devouring her.

She was trembling uncontrollably, parting her lips beneath the firm pressure of his, opening her mouth to the gentle probing of his tongue. A whispered, shuddering sigh escaped her as he moved his mouth from hers and began to kiss a path downwards to the angle of her jaw and her earlobe, and the hand that had been resting on her hip slid across her midriff, making her quiver and gasp as the feelings that had haunted her unsettled dreams since that night at Balfour zigzagged through her again.

He laughed softly, a warm breath that fanned her ear and spread goose bumps over her skin as he straightened up and took her chin between his fingers, tilting her face up to his so that she had no alternative but to look into his eyes.

It was as if the sun had gone out. They were as dark and cold and empty as a moonless midnight sky.

'I thought as much,' he murmured in a voice that sent shivers down her spine. 'Beneath that prim exterior you're human too, Miss Balfour.'

Emily jerked backwards, blinking dumbly, her head reeling as sense returned and she realised that she'd just walked right into the trap he'd sprung for her. 'How could you?' she whispered, shrinking away from him, pulling the robe around her as if it were a suit of armour. 'You did that on purpose. You manipulated me. You made me—'

'*Made* you? No. I merely showed you how easy it is to be led into temptation. Just remember that before you stand in judgement of others.'

He turned and walked across the room in the direction of the French doors. Emily ducked her head, gritting her teeth against the tears of shame and fury that burned like red-hot needles behind her eyes, just willing him to be gone and leave her alone with her humiliation and her hot, shameful longing.

'I wouldn't have slept with you,' she hissed. 'I wouldn't have let you go that far.'

He reached the door to the terrace and Emily felt a chill blast of night air as he pulled it open, and caught the feral scent of damp earth and grass beneath the delicate perfume of lilacs. Pausing he looked back at her, and for a moment she caught something like despair on his face.

'I wouldn't have tried to,' he said wearily, and then he was gone.

CHAPTER FOUR

IT WAS a spectacular sunrise.

Luis sat at the window of his suite watching the stars fade as a warm-pink blush crept tentatively into the sky from the east. He had given up on sleep and got up when it was still velvet dark, and in those dead hours it had seemed almost unimaginable that the cold and shadowed landscape before him would ever feel the sun's warmth again.

But gradually, inch by inch, the sleeping garden was washed with the watery rose light of the new day, softened by pearly mist. Many people would probably see it as a beautiful symbol of hope, Luis thought acidly. To him it was just another reminder that there was no let-up. No escape. Life just continued, relentlessly, whether you wanted it to or not.

Whether you deserved it or not.

There was a discreet knock on the door, and Tomás came in bearing coffee and a selection of newspapers.

'Morning, sir. I take it you slept well?'

Picking up yesterday's paper from Santosa Luis kept his expression neutral and didn't bother him with the truth. The night was over. Now he had to get through the day ahead.

'Brilliantly, thank you, Tomás,' he said blandly, scanning the headlines. 'Now, what exciting engagements do we have to look forward to today?'

Tomás consulted the printed itinerary on the top of his ubiquitous clipboard. 'Well, sir, there's nothing planned for the morning, but this afternoon you're scheduled to make brief visits to a mother-and-toddler group in South East London, a charity that provides sports opportunities for children in the care system, and a day-care centre for elderly people.'

'What fun. Talking of which, how's my father?'

Tomás shifted uncomfortably in his seat. 'I was just coming to that, sir. I spoke to his private secretary late last night and the news wasn't terribly good, I'm afraid to say.'

Luis looked up from the paper. 'Why didn't you tell me?'

'Nothing to bother you with, sir.' Tomás's words were intended to soothe, but the note of anxiety in his voice rather spoiled the effect. 'The king was admitted to hospital last night because he had had a little difficulty in breathing, but his doctor assured me he was comfortable and sleeping peacefully by the time I called. But it did make me think that we should perhaps think about returning to Santosa earlier than planned. Josefina in the press office is delighted at the success of the trip and the level of positive publicity it's generated, however—' Tomás hesitated, pressing a finger to his lips thoughtfully before adding '—she feels now that it would be counter-productive for you to be away from Santosa when the His Majesty is clearly unwell.'

Luis took a swig of coffee and set his cup carefully down on its saucer before speaking. 'Do the public know how ill my father is?'

'No, sir. It's been reported that he has spent some time in hospital, and the press office have made a vague statement about "tests" but no official announcement has been made to the effect that the king is…'

'Dying.'

'That's right, sir.' Tomás flinched at the brutality of the word. Or at the brutality of the way Luis spoke it. 'Josefina feels that this isn't the right time to make that kind of statement, what with the celebrations for His Majesty's Silver Jubilee only a matter of weeks away and everything else so…unresolved.' He trailed off, clearing his throat and ostentatiously leafing through the sheaf of papers on his clipboard.

Luis smiled sardonically, picking up the newspaper again and turning to the sports pages at the back. 'Don't worry, Tomás. I understand what you're saying. If the public got wind of the fact that King Marcos Fernando was about to die and pass the crown on to the notorious black sheep of the Cordoba dynasty there would be revolution on the streets of Santosa. Is that it?'

'Of course not, sir,' Tomás said, quickly and hugely unconvincingly. 'It's just that we need to do a little bit more work on your image before the public are ready to accept you as a successor to your father. As you know, your father is deeply loved by the people, and a twenty-five-year reign was always going to be a hard act to follow, even by…'

He stopped abruptly.

There was a moment of silence, and then Luis finished the sentence for him. 'Even by Rico.' His heavily ironic drawl was edged with a bitter edge of despair. Tossing the paper aside he got up and went to stand at the window, gazing out unseeingly over the exquisitely landscaped garden.

The sun was up now in a sky the same colour as the swimming pool that glittered beyond the beech hedge to his right. 'But there we have the problem, don't we?' he went on bleakly. 'If even my noble brother would find it hard to please the people of Santosa, what the hell chance do I have?'

'Every chance, sir.' Tomás came to stand beside him. 'You've made a great start in changing the way the public sees you. Now we just have to capitalise on that and keep up the good work so that—when the time comes— the public will see you as a caring, responsible monarch.'

Luis laughed hollowly. 'Great idea. And how do you propose we perform that little miracle?'

Tomás opened his mouth to speak, but at that moment their attention was simultaneously drawn by a movement below. Emily Balfour emerged onto the terrace and walked across to the stone balustrade that separated it from the lawn beyond. She was wearing the clothes she'd arrived in last night, minus the black tights, and Luis found his gaze drawn to her bare feet. An emotion he couldn't quite identify stirred somewhere deep inside him.

'Miss Balfour seems like a very sweet girl, sir,' Tomás said quietly.

Luis glanced at him. 'Is that just an idle observation, or does it have some relevance to the conversation we're having?'

Tomás's tone was carefully neutral. 'I was just wondering, sir—and without wanting to pry—is there anything of a romantic nature between you? Security informed me that you were back in your room early last night…'

'Nothing happened,' Luis said tonelessly, watching as Emily leaned her elbows on the balustrade. The morning sun gleamed on her polished mahogany hair, and as she tilted her face up to it, he saw her expression of absolute seriousness. She looked as cool and remote as a Victorian angel, and he remembered the fragility of her body as he lifted her out of the bath. 'As you say, Miss Balfour is very sweet, which makes her of limited interest to me.'

Her or anyone else, he thought blackly. Those days were over.

'Good.'

Luis raised an enquiring eyebrow. 'Tomás?'

'What we need is someone to provide a diversion, sir. Someone to absorb some of the media scrutiny, if you like, in a way that would reflect positively on you. But it would be better if it was someone with whom you have no genuine romantic attachment, to avoid unnecessary upset.'

'When she's no longer needed, you mean?' Luis said acidly.

'Essentially, sir, yes,' Tomás conceded. 'When the time eventually comes for you to marry and we need to begin to introduce the future Queen of Santosa to the people. But until then—'

'Remind me who's in the running for that enviable position,' Luis interrupted coldly.

'Until recently there were two possibilities, the Duchess de Mesa and Lady Helena Maygrove-Carter. However, those photographs of Lady Helena dancing on the table in a nightclub have led to the feeling that she's not a good choice.'

'Funny. They made me feel exactly the opposite,' Luis drawled, his eyes still on Emily Balfour. She had placed one foot on the top of the stone balustrade and was easing gently into a balletic stretch, lying along her extended leg in an impressive display of suppleness. 'But in the meantime you're saying I should take Emily Balfour back to Santosa with me?'

'It's certainly an idea.'

Luis tipped his head back for a moment, thrusting his hands deep into his pockets and gritting his teeth against the curse that sprung to his lips at this intrusion of politics into his personal life. With every day that had passed in the ten months since his brother died he realised more forcefully what a charmed life he had lived beneath the radar as Santosa's 'spare' to Rico's 'heir.'

He was paying for those carefree years now, and he would go on paying for the rest of his life. But even the price of his own freedom wasn't high enough to make up for what he'd done.

'What makes you think she'd come?' he said hollowly. 'What's in it for her?'

'She seems to be having a difficult time at the moment, personally speaking. I gather that she's unwilling to return home to her family, but I can't help but think that her present situation is far from ideal. However, she's clearly someone who is motivated by a desire to help other people, so it's possible that—'

'She'd be willing to help me out by compromising herself to improve my tarnished image?' Luis's laugh was harsh in the still morning sunlight. 'I think you may be overestimating her generosity there, Tomás.'

Tomás flashed him a brief smile but it died before it reached his eyes. 'Sir, that wasn't quite what I was getting at. I entirely agree that Miss Balfour would be uncomfortable with the idea of being part of any deliberate deception—however, with a little help from the press office, the media might be encouraged to make their own assumptions when they see you together.' He paused, turning round and going back to the table to pour more coffee. 'It was actually Princess Luciana I was thinking of.'

'Luciana?'

'She's just lost her mother, as has Miss Balfour. It's my observation that Miss Balfour is perhaps the kind of person who would take comfort in comforting others, and Luciana—in common with lots of girls her age—has a keen interest in ballet.'

The spoon made a musical sound against the china cup as Tomás stirred cream into his coffee, otherwise the room was very quiet. Standing at the window Luis looked down to where Emily had straightened up and was now changing legs, hitching her skirt up as she placed the heel of her other foot on top of the stone wall and leaned forward to hook her fingers around her instep.

'Does she?' Distantly he registered surprise, but it was overwhelmed by the greater surprise of how extremely tight and lush Emily Balfour's behind looked from this angle. 'Is your wife still Luciana's nanny?'

'Not at the moment. She went on maternity leave just after Prince Rico and Princess Christiana died, which was difficult for everyone. Valentina says that the replacement nanny, a Senhora Costa, has worked for some of the best families in Brazil and comes with superb references, but her approach is rather formal which seems to have made Princess Luciana withdraw into herself. My feeling is that Miss Balfour might be someone Luciana would open up to. She's obviously very good with children.'

Tomás came to stand beside him again. Luis waved away the cup of coffee he held out. The way he felt right now it would probably choke him. 'You've thought this all through, haven't you?'

'I spoke to Josefina in the press office at some length last night, sir.' At least Tomás had the decency to look slightly sheepish. 'She thinks that Miss Balfour could be an extremely valuable asset to Operation Chrysalis.'

'Operation Chrysalis?' Luis repeated, his voice dangerously soft.

'The process of overhauling your public image, sir.'

'Chrysalis. I see.' Dear God. It was like some far-fetched sci-fi film where they kidnapped a public figure and replaced him with a brainwashed clone. 'And neither you nor Josefina see any problem with using Miss Balfour as a Santosan PR pawn?'

'I prefer not to see it like that.' Tomás gave him a determined smile. 'I think that we're offering Miss Balfour an opportunity that will be to her benefit as much as ours, Your Highness. As long as certain safeguards are put in place, to protect her welfare.'

Luis stepped closer to the window and put his hand against the pane. 'And what would they be?'

'Firstly that you don't sleep with her, sir.'

His fingers curled up into a fist, as if he might be about to punch it through the glass. 'I think I can just about manage to restrain myself,' he said sardonically. After all, he'd resisted more tempting bodies than hers in the past ten months. 'And secondly?'

A moment passed before Tomás answered the question. When he did his voice was oddly subdued. 'We absolutely cannot put her in a position where she could be emotionally compromised. So you must be careful—very careful—not to let her fall in love with you.'

Luis gave a harsh, hollow laugh. 'Given the way that she feels about me I don't think that there's any danger of that whatsoever. The main difficulty will be getting her to agree to come to Santosa with me. As you've got the rest of it all worked up, perhaps you could turn your brilliant mind to that, Tomás?'

'That's easy, sir. Just do what you do best.'

Luis gave a twisted smile. 'But since seducing her is not an option—?'

'I was talking about charm, sir. You're a prince, remember? Be charming.'

* * *

Discipline. Focus. Control.

The words that had been her mantra all through the years at ballet school echoed through her head as Emily held the stretch and felt her muscles protest. Closing her eyes, she breathed in the clear, cool, lilac-scented morning and attempted to let go of the tension in her shoulders from a sleepless night.

Discipline. Focus. Control.

It's a shame those words hadn't been echoing through her head last night when Luis Cordoba had kissed her, she thought bleakly. It was a bit late now. In fact, the words *stable door* and *horse* were also echoing around in the wake of *discipline, focus* and *control.*

And also, come to think of it, *ruthless, arrogant* and *bastard…*

How dared he take liberties with her like that? she raged silently, swinging her leg down from the stone wall and lifting it again in a high extension, holding her foot above her head. *Not only with her body, but also with her mind, playing some sadistic game to try to expose her as some kind of…of…*

Hypocrite.

The word dropped into her consciousness like a pebble into a deep, still lake.

'Bravo! If I had roses, I'd be throwing them at you now.'

With a yelp of horror, Emily let go of her foot and staggered upright, whirling round in the direction of that sardonic drawl. Talk of the devil. Luis was leaning over the parapet that surrounded the balcony jutting over the terrace in the centre of the house.

'I was just doing some stretching,' she muttered, wincing at the obviousness of the statement and turning her back so he couldn't see how much she was blushing. 'I didn't know anyone was watching.'

'Don't let me interrupt. Please, carry on.'

As if. 'I'm finished anyway.'

'Good. Then I'll join you for breakfast. I've asked for it to be brought to your room.'

She turned round, opening her mouth to tell him to get lost, but instead gave a gasp of alarm. In one fluid movement he had climbed over the stone parapet around the first-floor balcony and was lowering himself onto the narrow ledge on the other side.

'What the hell are you—? For God's sake, Luis, no!'

She clapped her hands to her mouth, stopping the anguished croak of her voice as she watched him slide down so that he was holding onto the edge of the balcony. For a moment his body hung suspended, swinging, his shirt rising to show an expanse of golden, well-muscled back before he dropped to the ground.

The breath whooshed out from Emily's lungs. He turned round, brushing the dirt from his palms as he strode easily across the grass towards her.

'Very impressive,' she snapped as he came closer, folding her arms across her body, as if that would contain the frantic banging of her heart. 'But couldn't you have come the conventional way, like any normal person?'

'I could, but I would have had to get Tomás to inform security and bring two personal-protection officers with me.' He pulled a chair out from the table on the terrace and sat down, and in the honeyed morning light Emily noticed lines of tension around his beautiful mouth. 'It makes spontaneity a little difficult.'

She frowned, suddenly taking great interest in her fingernails. She didn't want to feel sorry for him. She didn't want to feel *anything* for him. 'But presumably it's necessary—for your own safety,' she said crossly.

'Is it? I think that if someone wants to kill me badly enough they'll find a way.'

The sudden hollowness in his voice made her heart lurch and she realised he was thinking of his brother. The deaths of Prince Rico and the Crown Princess Christiana in a helicopter crash had shocked the entire world. She swallowed, trying to dislodge the hard lump in her throat. 'Isn't that all the more reason to be careful?'

Luis looked at her steadily, and gave a slow, twisted smile. 'No.'

For a long moment their gazes held. She'd decided, at some point while she'd been twisting between the hot sheets last night, that if she saw him this morning she would be icily polite but utterly aloof. The words drifted weakly through her head as she looked helplessly into eyes that were dark with emotions she couldn't begin to interpret. She opened her mouth to speak—to say something that would demonstrate her icy aloofness—but at that moment there was a knock on the door in the bedroom.

It broke the spell. Luis got to his feet. Dragging a hand through his hair he spoke with his habitual wryness. 'That'll be the trained assassin now.'

'I'll get it.'

Emily darted inside, glad of the excuse to escape, and the chance to recompose herself as the room-service stewards brought out trays laden with silver coffee pots and plates of croissants. She sat down and waited for them to withdraw again, before saying stiffly, 'I was so sorry about the loss of your brother and his wife.'

'Not as sorry as I was,' Luis replied, helping himself to a croissant.

The shutters were down again, his sardonic mask back in place. Determined not to let him see how much his flippancy shocked her, Emily tried again. 'You must miss him a lot.'

'You could say that.' Leaning back in his chair Luis tore the croissant open with long, ruthless fingers, exposing its soft inside. 'I'd give anything to have him back—' he glanced at Emily with a bitter smile '—so I could get on with my life as it was before.'

'Of course.' Frowning, she took a brioche. 'You're the heir now. I wasn't thinking of it like that.'

'Weren't you?' he said bitterly. 'I wasn't aware there was any other way to think of it.'

'Er…well,' she said with a small, artificial laugh. 'How about in terms of personal bereavement? You lost your brother and your sister-in-law. Your father lost his son, and your little niece lost her parents.'

'Thank you for reminding me.'

She shook her head, speechless for a second before stammering, 'Sorry. I—I can't even imagine what that must be like…' She stopped again, looking down at her hands. 'At least, I can—a bit. How old is she?'

Luis shrugged. 'Five…maybe six.'

'You don't *know*?' An image of her sister Annie's little boy appeared in her mind, and Emily felt her throat close up with emotion. Three-year-old Oliver was the darling of the Balfour clan—doted on by everyone. His birthday was a red-letter day in everyone's diary, an occasion of extravagant family celebration and an excuse for all the sisters to spoil him shamelessly.

'I'm not great with little girls.'

'No.' Emily speared a curl of butter from the dish and put it on the side of her plate. 'I imagine they're completely irrelevant to you until they reach the age of consent.'

Luis looked across at her with dark, dead eyes. 'You make it sound as if that's a bad thing, whereas I'd suggest exactly the opposite.' He smiled thinly. 'It's not that I don't care about her. It's more that I don't know where to start. I don't have anything in common with her. She likes…I don't know, pink ponies, and ballet…'

'Ballet?' Emily stopped, the brioche halfway to her mouth.

'According to Tomás. Valentina—his wife—is part of the nursery staff, or was until she left to have a baby. Apparently Luciana's ballet mad.'

He was pouring more coffee, and Emily found herself unable to take her eyes off his hands. Against the delicate white china they looked very big, very tanned.

'Does she do lessons?'

'No. She's always been ridiculously shy, but since the accident she hardly speaks at all. She wouldn't have the confidence.'

'But ballet would be good for her.' Emily sat up, snapping

out of the hypnotic grip his elegant, long-fingered hands had exerted over her a moment ago, suddenly alert. This was her area of expertise. Her passion. 'Some of the children I've been teaching at Larchfield have really come out of themselves since they've been learning—like Niomi yesterday. She wouldn't even lift her head and look anyone in the face when she started, but one of the first things you learn in ballet is to stand tall and hold your head up. Everything else follows from there. You should encourage Luciana to take lessons.'

Taking a mouthful of coffee he gave a swift, dismissive shake of his head. 'Security nightmare. I might take risks with my own life but I wouldn't put hers in danger. I owe her that much, at least.'

Emily frowned, not understanding. 'But couldn't you hire a teacher? Privately?'

He looked at her, tilting his head and narrowing his eyes a little before saying slowly, 'It's complicated. Recruiting people to work in the household is always a long and tedious process, especially where my niece is concerned. It would have to be someone pretty special, you see. Someone Luciana could relate to, who would understand the situation she's in…'

He trailed off. For a long moment the only sound was the innocuous singing of the birds. His coffee cup was cradled between his hands, and she was horrified by the tremor of bliss that threatened to shake her as she remembered the way they'd held her foot last night, stroking and massaging. She was aware of a creeping heat in the pit of her stomach, a gathering tension between her thighs… But then in some tiny corner of her rational mind realization dawned.

'No,' she gasped, her eyes widening. 'Oh, no— You want *me*—' Words failed her. She got to her feet, shaking her head as she tried to clear it, tried to anchor herself to sanity and reason. 'After what you did last night you're actually asking me to come back to Santosa and work for you?'

He got up too, his gaze flicking scornfully over the writing on her T-shirt. 'Wouldn't it be better than working in a lap-dancing club?'

She laughed shakily. 'No. No, I don't think it would. Because at least the men there don't bother to hide what they want.' She threw her napkin down and slid out from her chair. 'They don't play games. At least there I feel a hell of a lot safer than I do when I'm around you!'

His head jerked backwards slightly, almost as if she'd hit him and for a moment the blaze of emotion in his gold eyes almost dazzled her. But then he looked away, dragging a hand over his face as if to blank it out again. When he spoke his voice was cool and faintly ironic.

'Your honesty is startling. Now, perhaps I'd better take you back to London.'

CHAPTER FIVE

EMILY'S hand was shaking as she tried to get her key into the lock. Behind her she could hear the low, thrumming purr of the car engine.

Don't look round, she told herself desperately, gritting her teeth. *Just concentrate on opening the bloody door and getting inside where you can forget all about Luis Cordoba and his…his…*proposition.

The door opened and she stumbled into the dingy hallway. Instantly she was assailed by the smell of damp, stale air and overboiled vegetables, and automatically held her breath as she tiptoed quickly past Mr Lukacs's door towards the stairs.

'Is that you, Miss Jones?'

She froze for a moment on the third step, her heart thudding. *No*, she thought despairingly. *It's not actually. I'm not Miss Jones, I'm Emily Balfour—what the hell am I doing here?* The past twelve hours—the exquisite luxury of Luis's hotel—only served to make her more cruelly aware of the filthy carpet, the black halo on the wallpaper around the light switch left by dirty, anonymous hands. With a shudder of disgust she raced as quietly as possible up the remaining stairs and along the corridor to her room.

She'd done the right thing, she told herself fiercely. Mr Lukacs's house in Bedford Street might not be a palace, but at least she was living there on her own terms, without compromising herself or the values she'd already sacrificed so much to uphold. Teaching ballet to Princess Luciana sounded like a dream job on many levels, but it wouldn't be that simple. Not with Luis Cordoba around. He did things to her head and turned her into a person she didn't recognize and certainly didn't want to be.

Turning the key in the lock she slipped inside and shut the door softly behind her, letting out her breath again. For preference she would have continued to hold it, as the damp, mildewy smell was almost as bad up here, but although she'd learned to do without many things she'd considered essential in her old life at Balfour, breathing wasn't one of them. Suppressing a shudder, she tossed her keys onto the cheap bedside table and quickly crossed the horribly patterned carpet to the wardrobe.

She was late for work, which at least meant that there was no time to dwell on the clothes she had left behind at Balfour as she pulled a black dress off its metal coat hanger. Struggling out of her tights she was just about to take her top off when there was a knock at the door.

'Miss Jones?'

Emily stiffened, her eyes darting nervously to the door. It was locked, thank goodness. From the other side she could hear Mr Lukacs's heavy breathing as he bent to listen for sounds of life inside, and felt a fleeting moment of guilt. He was just a lonely, middle-aged man with no one to talk to, she knew that. It was just the way his small, damp eyes scuttled over her as he talked that unsettled her.

'Miss Jones, are you there?'

Uneasiness crept up the back of Emily's neck as, taking great care not to make a sound, she lifted her top over her head. Hopefully he'd give up and go away in a minute, she thought, tiptoeing over to the sagging chest of drawers and wondering how she was going to open them and get her underwear out without making any noise. The top drawer was broken so you had to wedge it shut in a certain way and then yank it out…

She stopped dead. The drawer was open a little way, its

broken front gaping, some of the knickers and bras spilling out. Had she left it like that?

The scrape of a key in the lock made her blood run cold and answered her question. In slow motion she watched the door open, feeling as if icy, invisible hands were gripping her body and covering her mouth as a bulky, lumbering frame sidled into the room.

'Mr Lukacs,' she croaked grabbing the top she'd just discarded and clutching it against her, she shrank backwards. 'What are you doing?'

For a moment she saw alarm flare in those tiny, furtive eyes. 'Miss Jones…I…' He held up the key. 'I thought you were out.'

Her heart pumped adrenaline through her shaking body, returning sensation to her limbs and her numb, horrified brain. 'Wh-what do you mean? If you thought I was out why are you letting yourself into my room?' Her eyes flickered back to the underwear drawer, but she swallowed back hysteria and forced herself to keep her voice steady. 'You have no right to come in here and look through my things.'

His black eyes slid away from hers. 'I'm sure I don't have to remind you that you're very behind with your rent,' he wheezed, shifting uneasily from foot to foot. 'So you can't very well talk to me about rights, Miss Jones.'

The apologetic note in his voice was horribly sinister. With his greying shirt straining across his dough-like stomach and his thin, greasy hair there was something pathetic about him, and Emily would almost have felt sorry for him if she hadn't been so thoroughly unnerved.

'No, well…' She swallowed. 'I'm sorry about that, but I'm on my way to work right now, so I can pay some of what I owe you…'

'*Some* of it? Oh, dear.' His beetle-like eyes had come to rest somewhere around Emily's midriff. Surreptitiously she edged backwards as he ran his tongue over his lips before continuing. 'However, I like to think that I'm a reasonable man, and in view of your…financial difficulties…maybe we could come to an arrangement. A *friendly* arrangement…' His eyes flickered briefly up to meet hers, and there was a hungry look in them that made Emily feel sick.

'No,' she said in a small, strangled voice. The wardrobe was right behind her now—there was nowhere left to run. He was too big to fight off, so she took a gamble on the only option left open to her. Standing as straight as she could she spoke in the chillingly upper-crust voice of her headmistress at ballet school. 'No. I'll make sure you get the money. Now, please get out.'

For a moment Mr Lukacs's face worked and she thought he was going to argue, but he seemed to think better of it and with one last malevolent glance he was gone. Emily managed to stay upright until the door had shut behind him, but then her legs gave way and she collapsed onto the sagging bed. In the mirrored door of the wardrobe she could see her face—a waxen oval with two dark smudges for eyes.

Shaking, she closed her eyes, dropping her head into her hands and holding her breath against a sudden rush of hideous, debilitating homesickness as she thought of her bedroom at Balfour. Vividly she could picture the sun pouring through the windows with their view out over the garden, the rose-patterned curtains, the bed with its little gold corona and white muslin drapes. Unconsciously she got to her feet, light-headed at the idea of walking out of this horrible house and going home. So what if she didn't have enough money for the train fare? All she had to do was go and flag down the nearest taxi and Oscar would pay when they arrived at Balfour. For the taxi and the rent she owed to Mr Lukacs…

Call me when you grow up.

Luis Cordoba's voice echoed in her head, just as if he'd been in the room and whispered the words tauntingly into her ear. She sank back down onto the bed with a moan of despair. Of course she couldn't go running back to Daddy and get him to make everything all right. She had to do this on her own.

Whatever that meant and whatever it cost.

* * *

The moment the car door shut behind him, Luis's smile disappeared as instantly as if it had been switched off and he slumped back against the seat.

According to Tomás it had been a successful afternoon. The visit to the mother-and-toddler group had passed off smoothly, apart from the moment when one particularly attractive young mother had handed him her baby to hold and he'd been so horrified he'd almost dropped it. Women thrusting babies at him had been a stock image from his worst nightmares for years, but luckily he'd managed to make a joke about it and hand it back quickly. The sports project had been better. Sport—the urge to compete and the natural compulsion to win—was something he understood. He'd been genuinely interested to watch the children. So much so that for a while he had almost been able to stop thinking about Emily Balfour.

Consciously anyway, although the little pulse of dissatisfaction, an uncomfortable sensation of having failed, still crouched in the back of his head like a migraine waiting to strike.

The car began to move, and with massive effort he raised his hand to wave to the small crowd of elderly people gathered outside the residential centre before pushing it wearily through his hair and exhaling through tight lips.

He'd failed Oscar. And now he'd seen where Emily was living he understood that he'd failed her too. *Deus*…the place where they'd dropped her off earlier was beyond belief. The only positive thing he could think of to say to Oscar about the house in which his daughter was renting a room was that it didn't have its windows boarded up, like most of the others in the street.

Guilt—his familiar companion over the past ten months— settled on the leather seat beside him, enveloping him in its suffocating embrace as he thought back to this morning. When she had refused his offer there had been a part of him that had been relieved.

Because she was right about him. She seemed to be able to

see through him, right into his hollow heart in a way that few other people could. What was it that Oscar Balfour had said? *She's good, through and through… She applies the same rigorous standards she expects from herself to those around her…*

And that was what had stopped him trying to change her mind about coming to Santosa. He was already perfectly aware of the coldness of his own heart, the blackness of his own sins, without having Emily Balfour pointing them out.

But that was before he'd seen where she was living.

'I think that went very well, sir,' Tomás said brightly, settling back into his seat and shooting a sideways glance at Luis. 'You certainly succeeded in charming the ladies. They were all eating out of your hand.'

'Nice to know I haven't completely lost the ability, then,' Luis said, staring moodily out of the window.

'Ah. You're still thinking about Miss Balfour? Don't worry, sir. We'll think of something else to help your image. You did all you could.'

'No. I didn't.'

Luis sat up, a muscle flickering in his cheek. 'We're going back to the community centre where she works. Forget charm. This time we do it my way.'

'Sir?'

Luis turned to Tomás with a grim smile. 'This time we try blackmail.'

Compared with the other stains on his conscience, it would hardly cause a shadow.

'No…!'

Kiki stopped, her custard cream halfway to her mouth, her eyes wide with horror. 'He actually *let himself into your room*? While you were getting *dressed*?'

Emily nodded miserably, taking a mouthful of gritty instant coffee. 'He has his own key apparently, and I have a nasty feeling it wasn't the first time…' She had a sudden image of the drawer containing her underwear, open slightly, its broken front gaping and the contents spilling out. She suppressed a shudder and took another hasty mouthful of coffee.

'Pervert,' Kiki said disgustedly. 'Oh my God, that is so creepy. I know the room's cheap, Emily, but really, you have to find somewhere else.'

They were standing in the kitchen at Larchfield. Or at least Emily was standing; Kiki was perched on the countertop, the packet of custard creams beside her.

'I know,' Emily said with quiet despair, gripping her coffee cup in both hands and staring unseeingly out of the window. 'But it was the cheapest room I looked at by miles, and I'm already struggling to afford the rent. I just didn't know… I never thought…' She shook her head, struggling to explain without giving herself away how little idea she'd had about the realities of living on the minimum wage. 'I had no idea how expensive living in London would be.'

Kiki regarded her thoughtfully. 'I take it your move down here wasn't exactly well-planned, then?' she said, through a mouthful of biscuit. 'Were things at home difficult?'

Emily nodded. She'd come to regard Kiki as a close friend, but they'd never discussed anything personal. For obvious reasons. Like the fact that if they did, Kiki would realise that Emily had been deceiving her from the start.

'I had a…disagreement with my dad. My mum was ill and I stayed until she died, but the day after her funeral…I…just couldn't be there any more, knowing what he'd done.'

'And what he'd done—' Kiki probed gently '—makes going back out of the question?'

Emily's hands tightened around her mug and she closed her eyes briefly. Cheating on her mother, fathering a child, *lying to them all* and expecting her to lie too…

'Yes. It's out of the question.'

Kiki sighed. 'I wish I could help, but we just don't have

the budget to be able to pay you for what you do here. I would if I could.'

'I wouldn't do this for money,' Emily said bleakly. 'I do it because it's the only thing that keeps me sane.'

'Well, that's another reason to hope we stay open,' said Kiki with a rueful smile. It faded quickly. 'So what are you going to do? You can't stay under the same roof as the weird sex pest, and if your wages won't stretch to somewhere decent...'

'There is one thing.'

Emily was looking out of the window again, a strange, blank expression on her face. Outside the day hadn't lived up to the promise of this morning, and along the street she could see the cherry tree she'd passed yesterday. Since then its extravagant froth of silken blossom had been stripped by the wind, and now it looked forlorn and ragged.

'Marry a millionaire?' Kiki suggested in a weak attempt at humour.

A car was drawing up by the kerb on the other side of the wire fence of the community centre—a huge, black, shiny car with tinted windows. Emily watched it dispassionately. Around here expensive cars like that meant only one thing.

'If you could find me one that isn't a drug dealer I'll consider it. Until then I have to be a bit more pragmatic.' Ruthlessly she pushed away the memory of Luis Cordoba and his tempting, tantalizing, far-too-good-to-be-true offer and said dully, 'My boss at the Pink Flamingo has offered me a dancing job.'

'Dancing?' Kiki's face fell. 'I take it you're not talking about ballet. Oh, Emily—you couldn't. You haven't said yes, have you?'

Emily's hands were shaking, making the surface of the cooling coffee in her mug quiver. 'I said I'd think about it. But actually, I think it's best not to.' She attempted a laugh, but it turned into a kind of strangled sob. 'After all, what choice do I have? The money would be twice, three times, what I earn behind the bar, and until Prince Charming comes riding up on his white charger—'

A loud knock on the door made them both jump. Kiki rolled her eyes impatiently. 'What do you want?' she yelled.

The door opened. Emily gasped.

Standing there, looking relaxed and golden and as out of place as a sunflower in Siberia, was Luis.

'Coincidentally, I want Miss…Jones,' he said, answering Kiki's question, but looking directly, unnervingly, at Emily. He was dressed in charcoal-grey trousers and a very pale pink shirt, the collar of which was open, as if he'd just discarded his jacket and torn off his tie. Suddenly Emily felt like she'd stepped out of the freezer and into a heatwave. 'I hoped I might find you here.'

'Your Highness…' Flustered, Kiki slid down from the countertop and executed a kind of awkward curtsy. 'I'm sorry—I mean, I didn't know…'

Luis ignored her. His eyes were still fixed on Emily. 'What's wrong?'

Emily took a hasty mouthful of coffee, aiming for a fraction of the nonchalance he conveyed so effortlessly. 'Nothing. I'm fine.'

He shifted his gaze to Kiki, saying coolly, 'Perhaps you'd like to explain?'

Kiki looked from one to the other, clearly confused and hugely uncomfortable. Her grasp on royal etiquette was shaky, but she was obviously of the opinion that saying, 'What business is it of yours?' to a prince wasn't really an option. Looking apologetically at Emily she said falteringly, 'Emily's having a bit of trouble with her landlord. He's this really creepy guy—and he…he's been letting himself into her room and—'

'Kiki.' Emily hissed. The pure, profound relief she had felt when she had first seen Luis standing there had lasted only a second, and now she had the feeling that she was in a small canoe on a fast-flowing river. His presence seemed to fill every corner of the tiny kitchen, his aura of effortless glamour and his dazzling good looks making it seem even smaller and shabbier than usual.

'And what?' he said, turning back to Emily.

'Doesn't matter.' she said curtly. 'What are you doing here anyway?'

'Looking for you,' he replied, leaning against the door frame and smiling easily. He was back to being the laid-back playboy she remembered—all signs of the tension, the despair, she'd sensed in him earlier carefully erased.

Emily gritted her teeth. 'Kiki, would you mind—'

'No. I'd like Ms Odiah to stay,' he interrupted smoothly. 'What I have to say concerns her too and I believe there's something you haven't told her.'

She felt as if the ground had just moved slightly beneath her. *The bastard. He was going to give her away. She was trying…she was trying so hard to survive on her own, away from her family and without her name, and he was going to turn the only friend she had against her. And why? As some kind of revenge for turning him down this morning? Or was this all about the fact that she'd turned him down before that? A year ago.*

She dragged her tongue over dry lips and gave him a look that was filled with venom. 'Luis… Your Highness…'

He raised his eyebrows and said reasonably, 'About our conversation this morning.' He turned to Kiki. 'I'm very impressed with what you're doing here, Miss Odiah. The performance last night was excellent, and it made me think of my little niece back home in Santosa. She's very keen on ballet, but terribly shy, and as I watched last night it occurred to me how much she would benefit from Miss Jones's tuition.'

Emily had never seen Kiki dumbfounded before. Working at Larchfield she was resolutely unfazed by violence, drugs, teenage pregnancy, self-harm and many of the more extreme aspects of youth culture. But she was clearly floundering now. 'Wait a minute,' she said in bewilderment. 'You've asked Emily to go to Santosa and teach the princess ballet?'

Luis smiled. 'That's right.'

Kiki gave a short, incredulous laugh. 'But that's—'

'Out of the question,' Emily cut in sharply. 'I don't want to leave here.'

'What? You're kidding, aren't you? I don't want to lose you but, Emily, this solves *everything*.' A smile spread across Kiki's face and she took hold of Emily's arms, her silver bangles jingling as she shook her slightly, excitement shining in her eyes. 'You can leave that horrible bedsit and tell your slimy boss to shove his revolting lap-dancing job up his—' She stopped just in time, and cleared her throat. 'Sorry, Your Highness.'

'Lap dancing?' Luis threw Emily a look of unconcealed disdain. She ducked her head.

'I hadn't said yes.'

'But you were going to because you didn't have a choice,' Kiki said happily. 'That's what you said a moment ago, but now—'

Emily felt like the canoe was hurtling headlong towards the top of a huge waterfall. 'But what about the children?' she interrupted, looking imploringly at Kiki. 'About Larchfield?'

'I've thought about that.' Levering himself gracefully away from the door frame, Luis reached into his pocket. 'I know it will be a blow to lose such a valuable member of your team, Ms Odiah, so I want to make a donation to the centre. Perhaps then you could hire someone to continue Miss Jones's classes…?'

Kiki's eyes widened cartoonishly as she looked at the figure on the cheque he held out.

You had to hand it to him, Emily thought dully. She was utterly outclassed and outmanoeuvred. That little hesitation before he said 'Jones' wasn't lost on her. He had her over a barrel and he knew it.

'Aren't you both forgetting something,' she snapped. 'I haven't agreed to any of this yet.'

He smiled lazily, his eyes glittering with menace. 'But I hope you will. You can think about it while we go back to your flat and pick up your belongings. I'm sure you won't want to stay another night in that horrible bedsit. I'll wait in the car, shall I?'

He went out and instantly the room seemed to darken. Emily

slumped forward, the breath whooshing from her in a ragged sigh. Stepping forward, Kiki took hold of her arms again, bending so she could look into her face. Her eyes were still shining with excitement. 'Hey—talk about Prince Charming! That's all your problems solved at a single stroke, and…and… crikey, Emily, he's absolutely *gorgeous*!'

Yes. He was.

And that was a whole new problem all on its own.

CHAPTER SIX

SANTOSA is an archipelago of twelve islands in the Atlantic, some fifty kilometres from the coast of Brazil. With its crystal-clear waters, exquisite white-sanded beaches and excellently preserved sixteenth-century Portuguese colonial architecture, the biggest and only inhabited island is one of the most seductively beautiful places in the world.

Emily shut the guidebook that Kiki had bought her as a leaving present. Oh, well, she thought, looking out into the hazy blue infinity beyond the window of the plane, if you were going to be miserable and lonely, you might as well be miserable and lonely in one of the most seductively beautiful places in the world.

Stifling a yawn, she leaned back in her butter-soft leather seat and stretched out her legs, taking care not to touch Luis's as she did so. As a Balfour she was used to luxury travel. Childhood holidays had been spent in either Klosters or on Oscar's island in the Caribbean, and flying in one of Oscar's private jets meant that queuing to get through security and waiting in crowded lounges for delayed flights were not part of the Balfour holiday experience.

And yet even Oscar's no-expense-spared attitude to travel began to look a little low-rent when compared to flying with the Crown Prince of Santosa.

But despite the jaw-dropping luxury of the plane she still felt pent-up and on edge, her brand-new designer trouser outfit as hot and restrictive as a suit of armour. When Luis had driven her round to Bedford Street he had taken one shuddering glance into the broken wardrobe and forbidden her from taking a single item. The next day Tomás had taken her shopping on Luis's orders, waiting in the shiny black car which was parked on double yellow lines outside the front door of Harvey Nichols. After the grim financial struggle of the past weeks, entering the gleaming, perfumed halls of London's most exclusive department store should have felt like a return to paradise but, aware that every designer garment had an invisible price tag that was nothing to do with the one displayed in pounds sterling, Emily had kept her purchases to a few businesslike basics. Clothes for work, not for pleasure.

Nothing as vulgar as money changed hands, of course. Upstairs on the designer fashion floor, each item she tried on had been whisked away from her by invisible hands and returned to her when she emerged, shrouded in tissue in shiny carrier bags. Emily found herself unable to meet the curious glances of the shop assistants as they handed them over. Despite the soberness of the clothes she had chosen she knew that they thought she was the Prince of Santosa's mistress.

Which was ironic, she thought with a stab of black humour. She must be the only woman in the world between the ages of eighteen and eighty that he was actively not interested in.

Almost reluctantly she glanced over to where Luis sat. He was completely absorbed in reading the sports pages of the Santosan newspaper, giving her the opportunity to look at him without having to endure the scrutiny of those golden brown eyes. He was obscenely good-looking, she thought, her lungs constricting painfully. Even unshaven, with his too-long hair untidy where he'd pushed his fingers through it as he read, he looked like a screen idol, relaxing between takes for some Hollywood blockbuster.

Restlessly she forced herself to look away, turning her body slightly so she was facing the window. She winced as pain shot down her arm from the tender spot where a Harley Street physician had given her last-minute injections. Yellow fever and typhoid, he'd explained smoothly as he'd jabbed the needle into her arm—nasty illnesses that could really knock her for six if she was unlucky enough to be affected.

Emily sighed, closing her eyes and shutting out the view of the ocean far below. There was something she was at far more risk of suffering from, and which had the potential to cause her much greater discomfort. But there probably wasn't an immunisation against the lethal attraction of Luis Cordoba.

Luis read the same line of the match report from Santosa's game against Santa Cruz for a fourth time. Somehow, completely unexpectedly, Santosa had won, two goals to one, but Luis had no idea how this miracle had come about because his attention kept wandering away from the page and in the direction of the sleeping girl opposite him.

Not that she looked much like a girl in that outfit, he thought acidly, giving up trying to read and tossing the paper down on the table. He'd sent her out shopping for clothes to replace the monstrosities in her wardrobe, and she'd come back with stuff that made her look like an off-duty nun.

His eyes travelled disdainfully over her sober black trouser suit. No one could say she wasn't going to be a suitable role model for Princess Luciana, but would anyone with half a brain buy the fact that there was supposed to be something romantic between them? She was as far removed from the women he was usually linked with as it was possible to be. Thank goodness Tomás had alerted him to the fact that she'd come out of the shop with suspiciously few bags, so he'd been able to ring Harvey Nichols's personal-shopping department and order some more suitable clothes in her size. The assistants had been delighted and slightly vindicated to be able to package up all the items Emily had flatly refused to try on first time round.

The smile faded, and he looked thoughtfully at her sleeping face. Her dark hair was drawn back from her forehead in a way that might have been intended to look sophisticated but which merely seemed to emphasise her vulnerability. With her wide-set eyes closed, that incredible Balfour blue hidden, her face was oddly bleached of colour, giving her the appearance of a girl in a Victorian sepia-tinted photograph. His gaze lingered curiously on her lips, which were about the only part of her you could describe as plump....

He looked quickly away, shifting irritably in his seat as razor blades of forbidden desire cut through him. *Deus*, this self-imposed celibacy was doing unpleasant things to his head, and his body.

But of course that, he thought bitterly, was entirely the point of any punishment. It made you focus on your crime and repent.

Tomás appeared beside him. 'We'll be landing in a few minutes, Your Highness. Welcome home.'

Luis nodded, taking a deep breath in as the usual feeling of claustrophobia descended on him. 'Home,' he echoed ironically. 'Isn't that supposed to be where you can relax and be yourself?'

Tomás threw him a rueful look. 'Very funny, sir.' He nodded in Emily's direction. 'Would you like me to wake Miss Balfour?'

'No. I'll do it.'

Tomás wasn't the only one who was surprised by the sharpness of his reply. *Anyone would think I want an excuse to touch her,* Luis sneered inwardly, moving round the table so he was sitting beside her. Her head was tilted to one side, exposing the long sweep of her pale, delicate neck, and his gaze travelled along it, from the sculpted hollow at the angle of her jaw to the place where it disappeared beneath the stiff fabric of her jacket. However, his imagination didn't stop there. Eagerly it filled his head with images of the supple, girlish body under the grown-up clothes. The small breasts that he'd seen when he'd lifted her from the bath…the concave midriff and narrow hips…

Tomás's quiet voice broke into his thoughts. Fortunately.

'I just had a call from Josefina in the press office, sir. She's tipped off her contacts about your arrival, so we can expect a…*select* press presence.' Tomás glanced meaningfully at Emily.

'Let the circus begin.' Luis kept his voice very low so as not to disturb Emily, but the bitterness in it was still all too audible. 'So tomorrow morning Santosa will be waking up to front-page pictures of me getting off the plane with my new "love interest"?'

'That's what we're hoping, sir,' Tomás whispered. 'A feel-good story, to divert attention away from the less happy news of His Majesty's illness. So perhaps if you just bear that in mind as you walk to the car with Miss Balfour…?'

'What, and ravish her on the tarmac, just to get the message across?'

'Oh, no, sir.' Straightening up, tugging his cuffs smartly into place beneath the sleeves of his jacket, Tomás's tone was brisk. 'We're trying to reinvent your image, remember? This isn't about sex, it's about showing that you've put those days behind you. Presenting you as a sensitive, honourable, caring prince.'

Letting his head fall back against the seat, Luis laughed. It was a harsh, joyless sound. 'Tell me, Tomás. Does any of this ever strike you as wrong?'

'*Wrong*, sir? What could be wrong with that?'

'That in order to appear decent I have to lie? In order to appear honourable I have to use people?'

'It's part of the job, sir,' Tomás said simply, looking out of the window. 'You're doing it for the monarchy. For Santosa. Ah. We'll be landing directly. You'd better wake up Miss Balfour.'

It was dark, and Emily was dancing.

It felt good as her body took the familiar positions—neat, tight, controlled—but something was wrong, and as she raised her leg in a *passé* she realised that instead of ballet shoes she was wearing high heels.

She faltered, teetering dangerously as the darkness around her was filled with a loud roaring sound, and she was suddenly sickeningly aware that she standing on a very small platform, high, high up. Someone was holding her, with strong hands that were making warmth spread through her muscles, melting them and turning her body boneless and languid. She stiffened against them, knowing that she had to keep dancing, had to keep her body taut and hold those rigid positions, because if she didn't she would fall into the void, but it was no good. However much she tried to resist, the warmth was seeping through her, and she was melting, unable to stop herself, and falling, falling, falling…rushing downwards…hurtling through space….

There was a jolt. Emily's eyes flew open.

Luis's face swam in front of her, and for a moment the warmth washed through her again as she looked into the golden pools of his eyes. It was his hands on her shoulders, holding her, his thumbs gently massaging her collarbones.

She sat up. The plane had landed, she realised groggily. That explained the sensation of falling, although not why her stomach still had that feeling you get in a lift, speeding upwards.

'We're here,' Luis said tonelessly, letting her go.

Emily blinked, trying to drag her unwilling brain back to consciousness. How typical that after two nights in the hotel where sleep had proved irritatingly elusive, it had claimed her now with such undignified thoroughness. God, she'd probably snored. Or had her mouth ridiculously open for the past two hours.

'This is Santosa?' she muttered, bowing her head as she fumbled with her seat belt.

'Yes. There's a car waiting to take us to the palace.' Luis had got to his feet and he towered over her so that she felt dizzy just looking up at him. Instead she focused on his hand, hanging loosely at his side, which was right in line with her gaze. His skin was smooth and tanned to the colour of golden syrup and his fingers were long, but broad and unmistakably strong.

She shivered, the dream still vivid in her head, her body still tingling with sensations that were half remembered, half imagined.

Hastily she got to her feet as he stood back to let her go ahead of him into the aisle. At the door of the plane the damp heat hit her. It was like walking into the steam room in the pool complex at Balfour, and that combined with standing up so quickly after being deeply asleep made the blood rush from her head. She faltered on the stupid high heels she'd hoped would make her seem more grown-up, gripping the hand rail for support. And then Luis's arm snaked round her waist.

'All right?'

She nodded, not letting herself lean against him. 'Stood up too quickly,' she gasped. 'And the heat…'

They reached the bottom of the steps, but he didn't loosen his grip on her waist. Instead she felt his other hand move to the front of her jacket, his fingers working deftly at the buttons.

'What are you doing?' Looking up at him she made to pull away but he held her tighter, pulling her into his body as he freed the last button and threw open her jacket.

'Cooling you down,' he said gruffly. 'You're way too hot.'

If the heat of the day had felt intense before, it was nothing compared to the molten lava of desire that erupted inside her, flowing through her veins so her whole body glowed with it. Oh, God, this was what she'd feared. This was the reason why she'd turned down this job, because she knew she didn't have the sophistication or the defences to withstand his careless, arrogant flirting.

But he didn't look arrogant now. His face bore none of that sardonic mockery she'd seen so often, and there was a stillness about him that made her stomach turn over. For a heartbeat neither of them moved. His eyes were hidden behind aviator sunglasses which disconcertingly mirrored Emily's own face back at her, but she was barely aware of that because all she could focus on with any clarity was his mouth. The way his top lip rested on the fuller bottom one—the sharp indentation at its centre, and the slight sheen of sweat on his skin.

The sticky heat ebbed around them, giving the day a strange, slow-motion feel, like swimming through honey. Still drugged with sleep, Emily found herself remembering how it felt to be kissed by that mouth, unconsciously parting her lips and letting her tongue move over them as a breathy sigh escaped her....

He froze, and in the split second before his mouth came down on hers she glimpsed an expression on his face that was almost like pain. And then she was melting into him and he was kissing her with an urgency that was utterly at odds with his habitual insouciance. His arm was still around her waist, holding her up, and he slipped his other hand beneath her jacket, moving up over her ribs. Forked lightning zigzagged through her, nearly splitting her in two, as he brushed her breast, bare beneath the thin silk of her rose-pink camisole.

A tremor went through him, and for a moment the kiss went from urgent to almost savage. It was as if he was acting against his will, but was powerless to do anything to stop. And then he was pulling himself away, straightening up, setting her back on her feet again without his arms to hold her up.

Behind him, Tomás was coming down the steps of the plane, his expression thunderous.

'Your Highness, the car is waiting.'

In the car it was cool again. Emily felt the air conditioning turn the sweat in the small of her back to ice water and bring some sense back into her feverish brain. They began to glide smoothly forward across the tarmac and she watched the plane that had brought them from London and familiarity getting smaller as they left it behind.

She didn't dare look at Luis, slumped at the opposite side of the seat. Everything that she had been afraid of was happening already and she'd only got off the plane a few minutes ago, she thought despairingly. Her hands tightened around the guidebook she still held and she looked out of the window. They were driving along a road flanked by palm trees and a few low houses in shades straight from a child's paintbox. Even the flowers in the window boxes were unfamiliar—exotic splashes of scarlet and magenta and egg-yolk yellow that she didn't recognise as being like anything from home.

But that wasn't surprising. Nothing here was like home. Even she was different.

'I shouldn't have done that. I'm sorry.'

Startled, she looked round. Luis was watching her, his eyes hooded and his face grim.

The apology took her completely by surprise. She had expected the same cold lack of remorse as he'd shown in the hotel and had been ready with the convenient indignation, but the bleakness in his tone made it all dissolve into ashes.

'No, please…it was my fault too. I—' She broke off just in time, biting back the words that were in danger of tumbling out of her mouth. *I wanted it.* 'I was still half asleep,' she finished weakly.

He sighed. 'Even so. It was…wrong.'

Was it? A cold, heavy sense of disappointment, of desolation, settled in the pit of her stomach and she turned to stare unseeingly out into the green, unfamiliar landscape. *How could it be wrong when it felt so right?* Impulsively she opened her mouth to say this, but one glance at his face made the words dry up and lodge in her throat.

In profile he looked as if he'd been carved from stone. Cold, hard, utterly emotionless—a tombstone effigy of the man who had kissed her with such violent passion only a few minutes ago.

But maybe he wasn't kissing *her*, she thought as icicles dripped down her spine. She'd just been *there*.

The silence fell over them like a suffocating blanket. Gradually she became aware that she was gripping the guidebook on her knee so hard that her fingers had gone numb. She flexed them painfully back into life, and opened the book, desperate for some escape from the humiliating realization that Luis had kissed her because she was convenient, because she was a female pair of lips and he was bored and frustrated and because that was what he did. The history of Santosa was as good a diversion as any.

Portuguese explorers discovered Santosa by mistake when they were attempting to return home from their voyage around the new world. The ships, weighed down with cargoes of brazilwood, floundered on the rocky cliffs on the south-west point of the island and many sailors were lost. However, one of the survivors was Henrique Cordoba, Duke of Santosa—a flamboyant nobleman, notorious rake and favourite of the king, who had been sent on the voyage to escape gambling debts and a series of scandals involving the wives of other high-profile members of the court.

It must be a family trait. She turned the page, and felt the breath catch in her throat as she found herself looking straight into familiar, laughing golden eyes.

The Santosan royal family today, said the caption underneath. *King Marcos Fernando and his sons, the Crown Prince Henrique and Prince Luis.*

The photograph had been taken some years ago, she realised with a lurch of her heart. Luis's face was younger, more open, with none of the hardness and cynicism that were etched into it today. His smile was wide and untainted by irony, and standing shoulder-to-shoulder with his brother he looked heart-stoppingly handsome.

Her gaze shifted to Rico. His colouring was darker than Luis's, his hair shorter. He looked quieter and, compared with Luis's dazzling charisma, almost severe.

'What are you reading?'

'Nothing.' She tried to shut the book, but he was too quick for her. Taking it from her he glanced at the cover, and then turned back to the page she'd been reading. His expression hardened as he saw the photograph, but she watched his lip curl as he read out a passage from beneath it. *'The present monarch, King Marcos Fernando, enjoys a level of popularity amongst his people that is almost unique. His eldest son, Henrique, known as Rico, has been groomed all his life to one day take his father's place on the throne, and is held in high regard and great affection by the Santosan people.* Oh, dear,' he said scathingly. 'Not the most up to date edition, is it?'

'It was a present from Kiki.'

'Very thoughtful. Clearly she didn't think I'd be much of a tour guide, but I'll do my best. Look—here we are approaching the gates to the palace, home of what *used* to be one of the most popular royal families in the world.'

His tone was mocking but Emily felt her insides freeze as she saw the chips of ice in his eyes. Mutely she turned her head away, gazing out of the window at the imposing stone gateway that loomed up ahead of them.

The car slowed and the sun was blotted out as they passed beneath it. Guards stood aside, their faces blank beneath their helmets, guns braced across their chests. Glancing upwards Emily saw the savage teeth of a portcullis rearing above them.

'It's like a prison,' she joked weakly.

Luis didn't smile. 'Welcome to the royal household.'

CHAPTER SEVEN

JOSEFINA placed the newspaper down on the table and gave a brittle laugh. 'It wasn't quite the image we were hoping for.'

'Nice picture of Tomás,' Luis said blandly, glancing at the huge front-page photograph of him kissing Emily Balfour at the foot of the plane steps beneath Tomás's grim gaze. 'Very statesman-like.'

'Which, with respect Your Highness, is more than can be said for you.' Tomás looked pained. 'We talked about this. We're trying to present you to the people of Santosa in a new light, as responsible and—'

'Caring. I know. And there I am, being caring. Miss Balfour was far too hot and I was helping her to cool down.'

Tomás's eyebrows shot up. 'By undressing her on the tarmac?'

'By taking off that awful jacket, yes. I'd say that was very caring of me,' Luis said in a bored voice, turning the paper over and ostentatiously flicking through the back pages to the football scores. Despite his outward display of nonchalance a pulse was beating in his temple and he could feel knots of tension tightening in his shoulders.

'But, sir,' Tomás persisted, 'I thought we agreed that you wouldn't—'

Luis laid down the newspaper with exaggerated care. His patience hung by a thread. 'It wasn't planned, Tomás,' he said through clenched teeth. 'It was just…'

What? a small voice in his head taunted. *Unavoidable? Irresistible? Inevitable?* Because that was how it had felt at the time. And if his own guilt and the ghosts of Rico and Christiana hadn't been able to stop him, then Tomás and Josefina and the dictatorial demands of the bloody press office had no chance.

'Sir.' Josefina's deliberately placating voice broke into his thoughts, dragging him back to the present. Across the table she clasped her hands together, her long, shiny, scarlet nails reminding him of the blood-stained talons of some bird of prey. 'Sir, I hate to discuss your private life like this, but—'

'Really?' Luis arched an eyebrow. 'I thought you loved discussing my private life. You've made a career out of it, in fact. You and many of the world's gossip columnists, tabloid journalists, newspaper editors and the entire Santosan government.'

Her painted mouth shaped itself into an apologetic smile. 'Well, sir, you must understand that it's now a political matter rather than simply a personal one. Unless we can persuade the people of Santosa that you've left the mistresses and fast cars and wild parties behind you, the Royal House of Cordoba's five hundred years of rule could be in serious jeopardy. The people want a king they can look up to, Your Highness. Someone... *regal.*'

'Maybe we should advertise for the position.' Luis idly coloured in the bikini pants of the winner of this year's Miss Santosa contest, who was staring mistily out from page three in her tiara and a sash.

Josefina stood, pacing along the length of the polished table and giving him a great view of her lush curves, encased today in a tight emerald-green dress. 'Sir, it's not a job. It's your heritage. Your birthright. Your destiny.'

Luis opened his mouth to argue, but shut it again, throwing down his pen and leaning back in his chair with a resigned sigh. What was the point? It didn't matter what Josefina called it, or how she and the palace press team packaged it; it couldn't alter the truth.

It had been Rico's birthright. Rico's destiny. It was Luis's punishment. His prison term.

He rubbed a weary hand over his face and looked up at Josefina with a chilly smile. 'Of course. Thank you for reminding me. So what do I need to do?'

'"The time has come for you to be married," the queen told the handsome young prince. "Tomorrow night, all the eligible young ladies from every high-born family in the kingdom will gather here for a ball, and you must choose your wife from amongst them."'

Emily paused, holding out the book so that the little girl could see the picture. Luciana was sitting at the opposite end of the window seat, her dark eyes fixed warily on Emily's face, but now she looked down at the book and edged a tiny bit closer. Encouraged, Emily pointed to the picture and said softly, 'There's the prince, in his smart clothes for the party. Isn't he handsome?'

Solemnly Luciana nodded. 'Like Uncle Luis,' she said in a voice so quiet Emily had to lean right down to hear it. 'Uncle Luis is the Prince of Santosa. He's handsome.'

Straightening up abruptly, Emily cleared her throat. 'Yes, yes, he is, isn't he?' she said brightly, picking up the book again and resisting the urge to hold it right up in front of her face so Luciana wouldn't see her discomfort. 'Anyway, let's get back to *Swan Lake*. Where were we…? Oh, yes. *Prince Siegfried was angry and frustrated. He didn't like the idea of marrying a girl of his mother's choosing, no matter how elegant her manners or how noble her birth. He wanted to marry for love. The queen looked sad. "You are a prince, my son, and a prince has many luxuries, but choice is not one of them. And neither, I'm afraid, is love. You must—"'*

'Stop whining and just enjoy the fast cars and the champagne,' interrupted a familiar ironic voice from the doorway.

The book jerked violently in Emily's hands and her throat closed instantly, stopping her midsentence. At least a dozen acerbic responses to his comment jumped into her head, but all of them died on her lips as she looked up and saw him coming towards them, his hands in his pockets.

'Hello, Luciana, how are you? I haven't seen you for ages.'

And Emily hadn't seen him since yesterday, which had been enough time for her to play down his gorgeousness in her mind and have a good go at fooling herself that kissing him had been no big deal. Seeing him now, shockingly attractive in a soft, pale blue collarless shirt and faded jeans, was seriously unsettling.

Luciana quailed a little, as if she'd like to hide behind Emily, but dutifully she slid down from the window seat and bobbed a small, shy curtsy before shrinking back again. A bolt of shock and anger shot through Emily, but Luis's bland smile didn't falter.

'Please, carry on with the story,' he said tonelessly. 'I'd quite like to know what happens.'

Emily kept her attention focused on Luciana. Someone had to, she thought stiffly. She'd barely met her, but it was obvious that the child was seriously troubled. No wonder. From what she'd seen so far it appeared that the royal method of dealing with an orphaned child's grief seemed to be to hide it behind etiquette and protocol.

'It's fine,' she said briskly. 'We can finish it later. I'm sure you'd like to talk to your niece, as you haven't seen her for a while.'

Just for a second she saw alarm flare in his eyes and felt a perverse sense of satisfaction. He could overlook her, and treat her as if she was insignificant, but she wasn't going to let him do the same to Luciana.

'What book is it?' he asked politely, looking down at her.

'Stories from famous ballets,' Luciana whispered, twisting her fingers together. 'Emily gave it to me.'

'Well, it was from Uncle Luis, really,' Emily said quickly. 'And all the other things.'

'Thank you, Uncle Luis.'

'You're welcome,' Luis said, raising an eyebrow at Emily. 'Other things?'

She lifted her chin and met his eye. 'Ballet clothes. Leotards and tights and shoes.'

'Proper ones, not just for dressing up,' Luciana added, pride momentarily overcoming her shyness. 'Ones that real dancers wear, like Emily.'

'So I see.' He looked briefly at Emily, taking in the soft grey footless tights she wore, the little plum-coloured wrap-around cardigan and short, fluid skirt. 'So that's what you bought instead of proper clothes when you went shopping.'

'Yes.' She hesitated awkwardly. 'But the things you ordered were waiting for me in my room last night. Thank you. You didn't have to do that.'

He made a small sound of impatience. 'Judging from the dreadful things I've seen you in so far, I'm afraid I'd have to disagree. Yesterday's funeral suit should be burned, and you can't go out to a restaurant wearing a leotard and tights.'

Emily got to her feet, not meeting his eye as adrenaline pumped through her. He kissed her when it suited him, and yet he could barely disguise his contempt when he spoke to her. 'Well, since I'm here to teach ballet, not go out to restaurants, that shouldn't be a problem,' she said with exaggerated courtesy, 'but thank you anyway. Come on, Luciana, shall we go down to the gym and get started on your first lesson?'

'Wait.'

They were almost at the door but the word stopped her in her tracks. She noticed the way Luciana's grip on her hand tightened when he spoke.

'Yes?'

She tried to keep her tone neutral, but failed spectacularly. The word might only contain three letters but every one of them bristled with defiance.

'Has someone shown you the gym?' he asked, crossing the room towards her. 'I understand from Tomás that a barre has been fitted for Luciana's ballet lessons.'

'Yes, thank you. It's perfect.'

'And your room? Is your room all right?'

She laughed, thinking of the suite she had been shown to last night with its own sitting room and little sunny balcony. 'You saw where I was living before, so, yes, thank you. My lavish suite of rooms is perfectly acceptable. Now, if that's all—'

'It isn't.' He came to a standstill in front of her, leaning against the doorway, his expression offhand. 'I came here to ask you to have dinner with me tonight.'

She raised her chin, trying to hide her shock. 'Is that a request or a royal command?'

He smiled, a thin smile that didn't reach his expressionless eyes. 'Would it make a difference to your answer?'

'Yes.'

He sighed, and suddenly he looked very tired 'Then it's whichever will make you agree.'

For a heartbeat she didn't reply. She was aware of Luciana's tight hold on her hand. But mostly she was aware of Luis—the now-familiar, perennially intoxicating smell of him, the dark smudges beneath his eyes, the stubble on his hard jaw. 'OK, then.' She spoke in a low reluctant voice, as if the words were being drawn from her against her will. 'If you're asking as a human being, then we'd like to, wouldn't we, Luciana?'

Emily just had time to register the flare of surprise in Luis Cordoba's topaz-coloured eyes before she tore her own gaze away and turned her attention to the little girl at her side. Luciana blinked, biting her lip, clearly unsure how to react, so Emily dropped down to her level, smoothing a strand of dark hair back from her face. 'It would be fun. We'll dress up in something nice, and Uncle Luis can take us out for dinner,' she said softly, taking hold of Luciana's hands. 'We can have burgers and chips and a cola float. Do you know what one of those is?' Luciana shook her head mutely. 'It's a fizzy drink with ice cream on the top, and it's my absolute favourite. What do you think?'

'It sounds…nice.'

Emily straightened up, letting her gaze skim over Luis's long legs, his hard stomach, as she did so.

'Thank you. We'll be ready at six.'

'Excelente.' Once more his smile stopped short of his eyes and his voice was cool and tinged with irony. 'It looks like I have a date with two beautiful girls. Even by my standards that's quite a result.'

CHAPTER EIGHT

LUIS would have said that his knowledge of Santosa's night-life was pretty much second to none, but the Purple Parrot was one restaurant that wasn't on his personal radar.

The manager, almost hyperventilating with excitement at having the patronage of the Crown Prince, had shown them to a table on the veranda over the beach as agreed earlier with palace security, and while Emily studied the menu with Luciana, Luis looked around. At this hour the restaurant was busy with families; highchairs were stationed at nearly every table and toddlers knelt up on chairs, eating with their fingers. Luis shuddered, grimacing slightly at the plastic palm trees that held up the raffia-fringed canopy above them, the soft-toy parrots and monkeys and snakes that hid in their branches. It wasn't the kind of place he'd usually choose to bring a woman for a date.

Not that this was a date, he reminded himself acidly. It was another duty; a PR exercise, order of Josefina and the press office.

He looked across at Emily. She was wearing a short indigo-blue cotton dress, presumably one of the things selected by the girl in Harvey Nichols. It was loose, falling in soft pleats from a low neckline and, unlike any of the other stuff he'd seen her in, it suited her to perfection. She looked young and incredibly pretty as she sat beside Luciana, her head bent over the menu, her ponytail falling over her shoulder and exposing her delicate collarbone and the back of her neck. The rapier-sharp arrow of lust that skewered him caught him off guard and made his breath catch in his throat.

Emily straightened up and smiled warily across at him. If she knew what he was thinking she wouldn't be smiling at all, he thought acidly.

'Thank you for bringing us,' she said with clipped English courtesy. 'It's a great place.'

'I might have known you'd like it.'

The Balfour blue eyes held his for a moment, the darkening in their clear depths showing her anger, but then they were hidden by a sweep of her dark, thick lashes as she looked back down at Luciana.

'Have you decided what you'd like to eat, sweetheart?'

Guilt came down on him like the night as he watched Luciana lean closer in to Emily's side, pointing shyly at the menu. Guilt was his default emotion as far as his niece was concerned, and from the moment Emily had added the little twist to his dinner invitation earlier he'd known this wasn't going to be a relaxing evening. But that comment about this being Emily's kind of restaurant had been below the belt.

Unseeingly he looked out over the beach below, where the fierce heat had gone out of the sun and it was beginning to dip down towards the flat sea. The truth was the strength of his response to her unsettled him, and it was as though he had to make jokes about her being a child to distract him from the fact that his body was all too aware of. Emily Balfour might have been a naive kid last year, but now she was all grown up and ripe for the taking.

By someone, he reminded himself sourly. Certainly not by him.

'…if that's OK?'

Luis shook his head slightly, snapping back to reality. Emily was looking at him from the opposite side of the table, her expression cool and slightly challenging.

'Sorry.'

'I said, we thought it would be good to get one of the big dishes, for sharing, if that's OK with you?'

'Fine. Whatever.'

As he motioned to one of the half a dozen waitresses who were hovering, gawping in open admiration, Emily clamped her jaw together and tried to squash the fury that was billowing up inside her. Dinner had been his lousy idea, so now the least he could do was try to cover up how bored he was. As the prettiest waitress virtually sprinted towards the table and gave a breathless curtsy Emily turned her head in disgust, following the direction in which he'd been looking a moment ago.

Ah. So that explained his utter lack of interest in her and Luciana, she thought irritably, watching two lithe surfer girls splashing about in the sea. She didn't expect him to be interested in her, not when there were so many gorgeous women around, desperate for the opportunity to be on the receiving end of Prince Luis's meaningless charm, but at least he could show a bit more interest in his niece, for pity's sake.

Determinedly blocking out Luis's voice as he talked to the waitress in husky Portuguese that made it sound as if he was describing the plot of an erotic film, Emily mustered a smile and turned back to Luciana. Her heart turned over. The child was obviously not used to being out like this and was sitting very stiffly, her hands folded in her lap, her eyes downcast. She might have been taught everything in the royal rule book about manners but someone had clearly forgotten to initiate her into the art of enjoying herself.

'Don't look now,' Emily whispered, 'but I can see something looking down at us from that tree behind Uncle Luis.'

Instantly Luciana lifted her head and looked anxiously up into the plastic palm tree. Seeing the furry toy monkey peeping through the branches her face relaxed into a smile.

'If I was an animal I'd love to be a monkey,' Emily rattled on. Anything to avoid having to listen to Luis flirting with the waitress. 'I bet they have loads of fun, swinging in the trees all day. What would you like to be?'

Luciana thought for a moment. *'Leão.'* She bared her little white teeth and held out her hands like claws.

Emily clapped her hands in delight. 'A lion!' It seemed an unlikely choice for a child who was as timid as a tiny kitten. But that, she realised, was probably the point of the fantasy. 'I can see you as a lion,' she said, very seriously. 'Especially as you have such beautiful, strong teeth. What do you think Uncle Luis would be?'

Male chauvinist pig is the obvious answer, she thought crossly as they both regarded him across the table. And then she remembered the night at Balfour when he'd stepped out in front of her from beneath the snowy blossom tress and pulled her into the shadows. A wolf. With his golden eyes glinting with wickedness he'd reminded her of the wolf in Red Riding Hood.

'Do I get the impression that you two are talking about me?' he asked dryly, as the waitress departed with a final coy curtsy.

Emily cleared her throat, which suddenly felt painfully dry. 'We're talking about if people were animals what animals they'd be,' she said in a ridiculous, husky voice. 'Luciana would be a lion.'

Luis's elegant, arched eyebrows shot up, indicating that his reaction was the same as hers had been. As he opened his mouth to speak Emily shot him a warning look, and he turned to Luciana with a nod of approval. 'Good choice. You've definitely picked the best animal to be. What about Emily? What would she be?'

Luciana pointed timidly up at the monkey.

Luis made a tutting sound. 'Oh, dear, Emily,' he said, looking straight at her in that direct, deadpan way that he had. The way that made you forget that there was anyone else in the room. In the world. Damn him. 'I'm afraid you absolutely could never be a monkey. They're far too undisciplined and uncouth. Sorry, but you'll have to think again.'

'I don't know, then,' she laughed nervously, trying to dispel the heat in her cheeks. 'What do you think, Luciana?'

Luciana's forehead creased into a frown again, but Emily was pleased that this time it was one of pure concentration, not of anxiety. Watching her, you could almost see the wheels turning in her head as she considered the matter. Finally she looked up at Luis and said something in quick, breathless Portuguese.

He nodded slowly, and replied in the same language. For a moment, listening to his velvety voice caressing the cadences of his native tongue Emily had to hold herself very rigid to suppress the shudder of helpless longing she could feel gathering inside. As the two of them carried on their conversation she battled to bring herself back under control, so it was a few moments before she realised that they were both looking at her. She glanced from one to the other in mock alarm.

'What?'

There was a twinkle of merriment in Luciana's huge, dark, chocolate-coloured eyes that Emily hadn't seen before, but which gave her a little thrill of pleasure. A little thrill of a different kind of pleasure than she got from the dull gleam in Luis's eyes as she looked across at him.

'We've decided what animal you should be.' He lounged back in his chair, his long fingers toying idly with the menu as he regarded her. 'It wasn't easy. Luciana suggested a gazelle, whereas I thought you'd make a rather good flamingo, with all those bizarre ballet contortions you do, but in the end we agreed that neither of those were quite right.'

A hint of a smile flickered at the corner of his mouth, and Emily found herself unable to take her eyes off his lips. 'Go on,' she said slightly breathlessly.

'Well, in the end, after much careful consideration and debate—' he glanced at Luciana, who clasped her hands together shyly '—we came up with the answer. You tell her, Luciana.'

'Cavalo! Cavalo!'

'*Cavalo?*' Emily looked uncertainly from one to the other. 'I don't know what that is, but I don't like the sound of it.'

'A horse.'

'A *horse*?' she repeated in mock outrage, turning to Luciana who had clapped her hands to her mouth and was giggling excitedly—a sound which made Emily's heart sing. 'You think I'm like a *horse*?'

Leaning across the table Luis took hold of her ponytail and ran his fingers through its length. His face bore that sardonic expression, but his eyes had darkened and gleamed like antique topaz. 'Absolutely,' he said gravely. 'A young thoroughbred.' She flinched as his he brought his hand to her face and stroked the backs of his fingers across her cheek 'Delicate, nervy, but all taut muscles and quivering energy beneath that restrained surface…'

Emily was transfixed. It was as if the touch of his hand on her cheek had cast some spell over her, and she was powerless to move. Or think properly. She could do nothing but gaze helplessly into those eyes while he added in a voice that was little more than a low murmur, 'Unbroken, of course…'

Adrenaline and indignation and stinging hot desire crashed through her and she felt her mouth open to protest at his audacity, but the waitress was coming back, balancing the tray of drinks expertly on one hand while she executed another neat curtsy, and Luis was pulling away, leaning back in his chair, his attention already somewhere else.

Discipline, focus, control. Gathering together the shreds of her equanimity, Emily forced herself to turn to Luciana, whose face lit up as the waitress placed in front of her an enormous drink with a cloudy head of ice cream frothing on the top.

'What is it?' Luciana whispered uncertainly.

'A cola float, as described by Miss Balfour earlier,' Luis replied with a faint smile. 'And since she said it's her favourite, I thought she might like one too.' He reached over to the waitress's tray. 'There.' He handed her a tall flute of golden liquid, topped with a scoop of ice cream. 'A champagne float. The grown-up version. Now you can't say I treat you like a child.'

Beyond the shade of their palm-tree canopy the sun had turned pear-drop pink in a sky the colour of parma violets, and the beach was almost empty. The tide was coming in, each successive wave wreaking further damage to a large and intricate sandcastle Emily had noticed earlier.

That's what's happening to me, she thought darkly, taking a sip of ice cream and champagne. Slowly, inexorably, her defences were being broken down, and although she knew what was happening there was nothing she could do to stop it.

Luciana touched her arm very tentatively, bringing her thoughts back to reality. 'Emily? We didn't think of an animal for Uncle Luis.'

'No, we didn't!' She forced herself to look at him narrowly over the rim of her glass. It wasn't easy. He was so heart-stoppingly handsome that looking at him directly was a bit like staring at the sun, and doing it now made her realise how much time she spent when she was with him trying to avoid it. 'Do you think,' she began slowly, 'that since you and Uncle Luis are in the same family he could be a lion too? After all, the lion is supposed to be the king of all the animals.'

Luis took a mouthful of beer and put his glass down, shaking his head. Suddenly all traces of laughter had left his face. 'Exactly,' he said acidly. Then he looked down at Luciana and gave a twisted smile. 'Luciana is Rico's daughter. She's a regal lion through and through. But me…' His laugh had an edge of bitterness to it. 'Not so much.'

There was a small silence.

'A tiger,' Luciana suggested. 'Uncle Luis could be a tiger?'

Emily put her arm around her and gave her a little squeeze. 'Good idea. Uncle Luis can be a big, sleek tiger.'

Watchful. Predatory. Beautiful. It suited him very well.

'Here's dinner,' growled Luis. 'Be careful or I'll eat it all up. And you too.'

* * *

They ate deep-fried king prawns, garlicky chicken, *acarajé* fritters and succulent chunks of tender steak straight from huge heaped plates in the centre of the table, accompanied by lots of French fries. At first Luciana was stiff with horror at the idea of eating with her fingers, but bit by bit, under Emily's gentle encouragement, she got used to the idea.

Luis was tempted to feign awkwardness himself, just so Emily would have to feed him little mouthfuls from her own fingers. But, he thought, staring moodily out over the darkening ocean, it would definitely test his promise to Rico if she did.

The pear-drop sun had fallen right into the sea now and the sky beyond the palm-tree canopy was a soft sherbet pink, dotted with the first tiny diamond stars. The beach was empty, the sea flat and mirror smooth.

A perfect evening.

Across the table, Emily sucked her fingers and leaned back in her seat. The pink light gave her skin a rosy glow, so that she looked like a poster girl for some miracle cosmetic cream. Some of his ex-girlfriends paid thousands to achieve the same effect, he thought, with a twist of wry amusement. Fruitlessly, of course.

'That was gorgeous. I think I have to admit you were right about the horse thing. I've certainly eaten like one.'

'The food was surprisingly good,' he said. And the company too. All through dinner Emily had thought up further variations of the animal game, until they'd each decided what colour, plant and type of car they'd be, and in one short hour he'd come to find out more about Luciana than he'd learned in five years.

She was drooping with tiredness now, only just remembering at the last minute to put her hand politely over her mouth as she yawned, and looking at her he felt the same old tightening in his chest. Guilt, but something else too. For a while he'd also forgotten to see her as an object, a problem, a living, breathing reproach. She was a little girl, and he liked her. In her solemnity and cautiousness she reminded him of Rico.

'I suppose we should get this little one back to her bed,' Emily said reluctantly, putting her arm around Luciana.

A fragile sense of something shared had grown up between them over the course of the evening. Luciana had been at the centre of the conversation—Emily had made sure of that—but oddly that seemed to have added to the sense of intimacy between them. He found he didn't want the evening to end.

'Would you like some coffee?'

Emily glanced up at him in surprise, and then down at Luciana. She was almost asleep, her head lolling against Emily's side. Gathering her up, Emily pulled her onto her knee and settled her there, safe and comfortable in the circle of her arms.

It wasn't guilt Luis felt in that moment, it was pure envy, and it took him by surprise.

'Well…' Emily said uncertainly. 'She's had such a lovely time—it would be a shame to rush back.' She looked up at him, and her blue eyes were full of questions. 'And coffee would be lovely.'

Luis nodded in Luciana's direction. 'Do you think she's all right?'

'I'm sure she is.' Emily's voice had dropped to a low, breathy murmur. 'Look, she's pretty much asleep. She'll be fine, although whether the fierce Senhora Costa in the nursery will be happy is another matter.'

Luis made a sharp, dismissive sound. 'I don't care what Senhora Costa thinks, and I'm not talking about tonight. I mean…' He paused, feeling the words dry and swell painfully in his throat. 'I mean, do you think she's all right…generally?'

'You mean, is she coping with losing her parents?'

'That's essentially what I'm asking, yes.' In the soft evening the words sounded harsh and raw. Luis realised that he was looking into Emily Balfour's clear blue eyes almost imploringly, and he turned away and stared out over the satiny ocean instead.

Oscar's words came back to him like a whisper on the warm breeze. *She's good, through and through*, and he felt them like a knife in the gut. He wanted her reassurance, he realised. He wanted her to say that Luciana was OK, because he wanted to feel better about what he'd done. He wanted her absolution.

'I don't know.' Her voice was very soft, but her words twisted the knife. 'She's very shy, certainly, but I get the impression that her reserve is more than just shyness.'

The waitress had brought coffee, he noticed distantly. The glass coffee pot stood in the centre of the table now, but he didn't bother to pour it. 'What do you mean?'

'Well, of course, I've only just met her, and I'm not exactly an expert on children—' she looked up at him through her dark lashes and flashed him a brief smile '—even though you think I actually am one.'

Luis frowned, too focused on what she was saying to pick up on the joke. 'But you think she's...troubled?'

'No more than any other child who's lost her parents so young. Tell me...' She paused, and Luis watched her gently twining a lock of Luciana's dark hair round and round one slender finger. 'How old were you when your mother died?'

Luis stiffened as a tiny bolt of shock shot through him at the question. Suddenly he was back in the hotel room in England, looking down on her as she floated in the bath, her hair floating around her pale, still face. With a sharp shake of his head he shoved the image back into the dark corner of his mind where it had spent the past half a lifetime. 'Much older than Luciana,' he said impatiently. 'Fourteen.'

'And how did you cope?'

He reached out and pushed the plunger down on the coffee pot in one vicious stabbing movement, making a little of the dark liquid spill out onto table. 'I did a lot of sport and discovered girls.' And along with girls, the amazing, anaesthetic qualities of sexual attraction, which temporarily blotted out unpleasant emotions, like sadness and loneliness and grief. Of course, now there was only guilt to blot out, but he had to do it without recourse to the old methods. 'I don't think either of those things are really an option for Luciana, so I don't see how this is relevant.'

'You didn't talk to anyone about it?'

He exhaled sharply, a gust of incredulity. '*Deus*, no.'

Lifting her head she looked at him curiously. Hell, she was pretty. Talking to her was the last thing he felt like doing. He wanted to silence her mouth with his and drag her off to bed.

'You make it sound like an outrageous idea.'

Suppressing a sigh of great weariness Luis splashed coffee into the two cups. The restaurant was quieter now; most of the families with young children had left, and now the tables were occupied by surfers who'd finished on the beach for the day and were relaxing with beers. Luis envied them.

'In our family it is.' He swiped away the coffee on the table with the side of his hand. 'Being a Cordoba is about saying the correct thing, not the honest thing. You can't change that. It's part of the deal.'

'Surely it doesn't have to be?' she persisted gently. 'There are lots of things that are beyond your control—like what happened to Luciana's parents—but you can influence how you handle those things. Help her to deal with it.'

Luis felt as if the world had stopped turning for a moment. There was a pounding in his head, a slow, relentless throb like the beat of a drum, or the toll of a funeral bell. Suddenly his mouth was filled with ash, so he took a gulp of his coffee.

'How?' he said tersely. 'How can I help her to deal with it?'

'You can talk to her about it—about them. And let her talk to you. I think that maybe the reason she doesn't talk much at the moment is because she knows she's not allowed to say the things that she's thinking.'

Luis turned away, his lip curling in disdain. There was so much Emily Balfour didn't know. So much he hoped she'd never find out. She was too good, too honest and straightforward, to understand that talking to Luciana about what happened was impossible. Unthinkable.

'You don't understand,' he said flatly, and was about to try to explain when a movement on the beach below them caught his eye. Not a person quite, but the distinct shadow of one, flickering across the uneven sand, betraying the fact that there was someone lurking beneath the veranda. One with a camera and recording equipment, he had no doubt.

Across the table Emily regarded him steadily. 'Try me.'

But already he was on his feet, pushing the hair back from his forehead, his eyes darting around the softly lit terrace beneath the canopy.

He'd lowered his guard. He'd completely forgotten Josefina and her bloody press contacts and for a moment he had just been himself. *Deus*, basic error. Maybe it was just as well the paparazzi had shown up or God knows what he would have ended up saying. Doing.

'Time to go.'

In one swift movement he was by her side, gathering up Luciana from her knee and into his arms. As he bent to pick her up he caught the soft scent of Emily's hair. She relinquished Luciana without protest, but glancing at her face he saw a dull flush of anger along her cheekbones.

There was no time to explain.

And what would he have said anyway? That the whole thing had been Josefina's idea, a royal photo opportunity set up to make him look better than he was? That was hardly likely to make her look upon him any more favourably.

'*O carro, por favor, Raimiro.*'

While they'd been eating his two bodyguards had been sitting discreetly at a table by the door to the main restaurant, but now they leapt to their feet. Raimiro was on the phone before he'd finished speaking, and with the speed and efficiency of long practice they were moving quietly through the restaurant to the door. Luciana felt warm and soft in his arms, and he felt a surge of fury and protectiveness as he held her head against his chest and wove his way quickly through the tables.

The car drew up as they emerged into the pastel-hued evening. He pulled open the door, shielding Luciana's face as he stood aside to let Emily in before getting in beside her. It all took just a matter of seconds. Barely enough time for Josefina's pet photographers to have picked up their cameras.

Emily's face was stony, but leaning back in his seat, Luis allowed himself a small smile of satisfaction. He'd acted completely on instinct, and for once it hadn't been for his own benefit.

It felt surprisingly good.

CHAPTER NINE

CONCERNS Grow for King's Health...

The headline said it all really, but just in case anyone was left with any doubts about the king's illness, the huge front-page photograph of a waxen-faced King Marcos Fernando slumped in the back of the car en route from the private clinic would have settled them once and for all.

Luis looked at the picture for a long time and, aware that Josefina was virtually combusting with the urge to speak, began very slowly to read the story too. He'd got as far as the bit about sources close to the king confirming that he'd attended the clinic for a series of tests when Josefina could hold herself back no longer.

'It really is *most* unfortunate, sir.'

'Absolutely,' Luis said gravely, setting the paper aside. 'Thank you for your concern. I'll be sure to pass on your good wishes to my father.'

At least she had the good grace to blush. 'Of course. That would be most kind, and *obviously*—' she stressed the word slightly, which ironically had the effect of making her sound even more insincere '—the King's personal health is the most important thing in all this, but my job is to keep an eye on the long-term welfare of the monarchy. Really, sir, it's very regrettable that the King's illness has been given such prominence at this stage. We had hoped that by going out with Miss Balfour last night—'

'Miss Balfour *and* Princess Luciana. It was hardly a romantic date.'

'Even better!' There was a clash of bangles as Josefina threw her hands up theatrically. 'A completely new perspective on the Prince—the perfect way to keep the King's health in the background *and* show the public your caring side! The photographers were strictly briefed to be respectful of the Princess's age and her vulnerability, sir, but in the end you hardly gave them a chance to get a usable shot. Which is why—' she didn't bother to conceal her exasperation '—*you're* relegated to one paragraph on the end of the story about the King.'

'Am I? I missed that,' Luis drawled. 'Oh, yes, here it is. *"One person who doesn't seem overly worried about the King's health is Crown Prince Luis. Instead of spending the evening at his ailing father's bedside he chose to go out for a fun dinner with his niece, Princess Luciana. This is the first time the playboy Prince has been seen with the daughter of his late brother, although this sudden interest may have more to do with the Princess's new dance teacher, Emily Balfour, with whom the Prince was spotted in a steamy clinch recently".*' He put the paper down. 'How cynical the press can be.'

'They have a job to do, sir. Just like I do. And just like you do.'

'The difference is they *chose* to be unscrupulous parasites and you *chose* to be an arch manipulator of the truth, whereas I…' He was about to say that he'd had his role thrust upon him, but stopped. It would have been a lie. He'd brought it on himself. And whatever other facts about himself he might allow Josefina to spin and remodel, that one was unalterable.

He sighed, suddenly feeling very tired. 'Anyway, I'm sorry to have ruined the master plan. Do you have any other ideas to transform my tawdry image?'

A look of immense relief settled on Josefina's expertly made-up face. 'Well, the first thing is to go and see your father—'

'I have,' Luis interrupted wearily. 'I spent an hour with him this morning.' For much of that time King Marcos Fernando had been asleep, and Luis had simply sat by the bed, looking down at the parchment-pale face, trying to reconcile the reality of the frail old man in the bed with the myth of the strong, infallible monarch in which the people of Santosa were so desperate to believe.

'A private visit is no good, sir.' Josefina looked at him as if he was missing something obvious. 'You need to let the press know that you're going, alert photographers and a news crew, and be ready to give a comment to reassure the people that the king is doing well.' She spoke quickly, ticking each point off on a scarlet-tipped finger. 'Also, I think we need to start publicizing the jubilee event more aggressively. It's only a matter of weeks away, and it will give people something to focus on and a reason to feel optimistic in these…uncertain times.'

Luis kept his eyes fixed on the potted palm behind Josefina. It reminded him of the restaurant last night and for a moment the memory of Emily Balfour's face, the sinking sun turning her eyes to violet and her cheeks to rosy gold. He'd joked so many times about her being a child—and why? Because of that night a year ago when she'd refused to succumb to his meaningless, empty seduction. Evidence if ever it was needed that she was wise way beyond her years.

'…but actually, I think that's the key.'

'I'm sorry?' Luis brought his gaze back to Josefina, wondering how much of what she'd said he'd just missed. He'd been so lost in thought she could have just informed him that she'd arranged for him to be fed to a cage of lions as part of the jubilee entertainment for all he knew.

'Princess Luciana. I think she's going to be a massive asset. I respect your decision as the Princess's legal guardian to keep her out of the public eye, but the jubilee would be the perfect opportunity to give her a more prominent role.'

'No.' Luis stood abruptly, disgust mixing with the same primeval instinct that he'd felt last night when the paparazzi had appeared. *An asset. Deus.* 'Luciana's too young, and far too vulnerable. She couldn't deal with the press, and she shouldn't have to.'

'With respect, sir, she's going to have to sometime. You can't let her grow up like some princess in a fairy tale, kept in a tower.'

'I'm not suggesting that,' he snapped. Or was he? Was his guilt over what had happened to Rico and Christiana clouding his judgement? What would they do?

As if she'd read his thoughts, Josefina said, 'Prince Rico was always most keen that she should grow up understanding the duties of her position. I know it's difficult, but I genuinely believe that she would benefit from this greatly. She already seems to have bonded very firmly with Miss Balfour, and since she's a trained ballet dancer…'

Luis shook his head, his mind was whirring. 'Wait a minute—what exactly are you suggesting?'

'The Brazilian National Ballet.' Josefina looked at him with a trace of exasperation. 'They're lined up to perform as part of the jubilee celebrations. And I thought that maybe Princess Luciana and Miss Balfour could be part of the performance.'

No.

The word sprung to Luis's lips, but got no further. What right did he have to dictate Emily's life? She was a dancer, for God's sake. He had brought her over here to use and manipulate her, and the least he could do was let her have the chance to do something she loved.

And as for Luciana… Hadn't he already had far too much influence on her life already? Hadn't his flawed judgement and shallow, selfish attitude affected her enough?

Down below in the courtyard the sunlight glinted off the polished buttons and gleaming rifles of the guards stationed at the inner gateway.

'What if Miss Balfour doesn't want to do it?'

'I'm sure she will, sir. I took the liberty of contacting the principal of her ballet school in England, to find out whether she was up to a major role. Apparently she's an extremely gifted dancer, sir—the star of her year. When she left last year her career as a prima ballerina looked assured, but her mother's illness seems to have brought it to something of a halt. The principal was clearly of the opinion that this was a travesty.'

Luis closed his eyes, picturing Emily on the rickety stage in that dingy community centre in her Pink Flamingo T-shirt, and the fluid grace with which she'd moved.

'The Brazilian ballet are doing *Giselle* on the mainland at the moment, and I've just managed to get tickets for you for Saturday night's performance. Why don't you take her, and ask her then?'

'Oh, that was brilliant!' Emily exclaimed, as she and Luciana finished going through the very simple routine she'd devised to introduce her to the basic ballet positions. 'Do you know, I think you're a natural ballerina!'

Luciana bowed her head shyly, but in the mirrored wall of the palace's state-of-the-art gym Emily could see her smile of pride. What she said was true though. Perhaps because of her shyness Luciana naturally had the upright bearing that made much of the preliminary stuff unnecessary.

Emily held out her hand to her. 'Let's have a little rest, and then we'll do some more work on those toes. If you're not too tired, after last night?'

Taking her hand Luciana shook her head fiercely. 'Oh, *no*. I'm not tired at all.'

Emily led her over to the bench along the wall and passed her a plastic bottle of water. 'All dancers have to drink plenty of water when they're practising.'

Luciana took a small sip. 'I liked the drink from the restaurant better.' The little frown line appeared between her eyebrows. 'What was it called again?'

'A cola float.' Emily laughed. 'But they're strictly for special occasions only.'

There was a small pause, then Luciana said, 'Last night was

a special occasion, wasn't it? I know it wasn't my birthday or Christmas or my grandpa the King's birthday, but it still *felt* like a special occasion.'

'Yes, it did,' Emily agreed quietly. It had felt like a special occasion to her too. The beach at sunset, the silly champagne float, the shared food and the game they had played had all made it feel special…. And Luis. Luis had made *her* feel special. She remembered the feel of his fingers sifting through her hair and the peculiar intensity in his eyes as he'd asked her what she thought about Luciana.

And for once he hadn't been cynical or mocking or taken the opportunity to tease her about being a child. She had had a kind of breathless, dizzying feeling that he was about to let her into a place that was as closely guarded as the inner sanctum of the palace. And then at the last minute he had withdrawn behind those thick stone walls and let down the portcullis, and the evening had been over.

She got abruptly to her feet, and strode over to the CD player. 'Anyway,' she said briskly, desperate to calm the sudden fizz and crackle of desire that had gripped her whole body. 'Shall we carry on? Now you've got the hang of the positions we can do some more advanced moves.'

Ultimately she just hadn't been special enough, she thought angrily, turning on the CD. Maybe the whole 'deep and meaningful conversation' routine was one of the many strategies in his seduction repertoire, and in the end he'd just decided she was too dull, too gauche, too *unbroken*, to be worth the effort.

Luciana had gone over to the barre and was standing there waiting, her body held very upright, her eyes fixed on Emily's face. Seeing the anxiety in them Emily instantly felt awful. She hadn't meant to sound so terse. Consciously forcing herself to relax she did a little pirouette and then swept down in a low bow.

'Would Princess Luciana give me the honour of this dance?'

The music was a plodding polka, intended for exercise work, but Emily swept Luciana up in her arms and waltzed her around the room, swooping and hopping until they were both breathless and Luciana was giggling uncontrollably. Neither of them heard the door open, or were aware that they were being watched, until they whirled round and saw the solid figure in a starched nurse's uniform standing squarely in the middle of the floor.

Emily staggered backwards, letting Luciana slide from her arms. The laughter on her lips instantly died as she saw the expression of supreme disapproval on Senhora Costa's face, which didn't alter as, with a rustle of starch, she curtsied to Luciana.

Emily felt her insides go cold.

'It is time for Her Highness's lunch and her afternoon nap,' the nanny said stiffly, taking Luciana by the hand and marching towards the door. 'In future, Senhora Balfour, I would ask that you could return the Princess to the nursery yourself at one o'clock sharp. The importance of routine cannot be underestimated.'

'I—I'm sorry…' Emily called after them, but as the door slammed in their wake she knew she wasn't remotely sorry about lunch or naps or routine. She was sorry for Luciana.

Viciously she stabbed the off button, and the music ceased. Emily tugged off her ballet shoes and threw them back into her bag, where they landed on top of the pointe shoes she had brought with her.

She paused, her heart still beating out a hard, angry rhythm. And then lowering herself down onto the smooth, blond wood floor she took the satin slippers out of her bag.

They were old ones—one of the few things that she had brought with her from Balfour, and the toes were frayed and worn. Picking one up she ran the tattered satin ribbons through her fingers and flexed the shoe between her hands so it was folded almost in half, thinking about when she'd worn them, to dance *Sleeping Beauty* in her final year.

Her lucky shoes. That's how she'd always thought of them. That's why she'd brought them with her when she left home, but of course by then their luck seemed to have deserted them. She shoved her foot into the left shoe, pushing her toes down hard to the block at the end, feeling the pain. Pain was part of ballet; she'd never been afraid of that—of the blisters and the blood, and the ugly, raw calluses.

Behind her the door opened. She looked round, but the tingling sensation in her spine had already told her who she would see. Luis's broad shoulders almost filled the door frame and the spotlights set into the ceiling of the studio shone on his bronze hair and turned it to gold.

'I'm afraid you just missed Luciana,' she said, turning away again and concentrating hard on tightening her pointe shoe. 'Senhora Costa took her back to the nursery for lunch and her rest.'

'It was you I wanted.'

His voice was perfectly neutral. So why did her heart feel like a rubber ball that had been bounced against her ribs? She took the ribbons of her shoe and crossed them tight across her ankle, winding round and pulling hard.

'What for?'

Footsteps on the wooden floor, coming towards her. She kept her head bent over her foot, but the hairs on the back of her neck rose as he came to a standstill right behind her. 'I just wanted to ask you…' He paused, and she lifted her head and looked into the mirror in front of her. Their eyes met, and Emily experienced the same sensation as you got when you touched an electric fence. An electric fence around a huge, black chasm, warning her to keep away from the edge. 'I wanted to ask you if you'd like to come—'

She looked swiftly down again. 'I don't think so.'

He came forward so he was standing in front of her, leaning against the barre. 'You haven't heard what I was going to say yet.'

'It doesn't matter.' She finished tying the ribbon around her ankle and tucked the knot in, neatly, out of sight. 'I just think that after last night it would be better—simpler—if we kept things on a professional basis. Could you please pass me the other shoe?'

It was lying on the top of her ballet bag. He bent and picked it up, but he didn't hand it to her straight away. 'This is professional,' he said absently, turning it over in his hands, feeling the hardness of the pointe. 'I was going to ask if you'd like to come with me to the ballet.'

Emily looked up, holding onto her bare foot. 'The ballet?'

'It's the Brazilian National Ballet performing.' He frowned, still looking at the shoe. 'I assumed that ballet shoes would be soft, but this is rock hard. Doesn't it hurt?'

'Yes, but you get used to it. After a while you stop noticing. Which ballet is it?'

A shadow of some emotion she couldn't read passed across his face. With a faint, twisted smile he handed her the shoe.

'I think it had a girl's name,' he said tonelessly. 'Beginning with *G*?'

'Not *Giselle*?' She couldn't quite hide the wistfulness in her voice, and swallowed it back as she raised her knee and eased her foot into the satin shoe. It was still warm from being held between his hands, and her foot flexed and pointed almost of its own accord, as if it remembered how that felt. Suddenly she was right back in the hotel room, lying on the bed while he cradled her foot between his palms, massaging her instep with his thumb…

He was watching her, his eyes opaque and gold. Every inch of her body thrummed with awareness as he nodded slowly. 'I think that was it. If so, is that a yes?'

The room was very quiet, and for a long moment the silence stretched and swelled as uncertainty and longing fought within her. She had told herself to stay away from him, to keep to the path and not stray into the woods, but after all this time the lure of the ballet was impossible to resist. She lowered her gaze, concentrating on tying the ribbons of her shoe. 'Yes,' she said in a low voice, as she stood and rose tentatively onto her pointes, bending each foot in turn and arching it hard against the floor. 'Yes, please.'

He levered himself off the barre and began to walk towards the door, suddenly businesslike and offhand again. 'Good. It's a week on Saturday. Someone will come and see you about clothes, just to make sure you've got something suitable. I'll see you then.'

A week on Saturday? Emily gripped the barre as a bolt of irrational panic shot through her, catching her completely off guard. 'I won't see you before then? Are you going away?'

He stopped in the doorway and turned round. He looked distant, controlled, perfect. 'No. I'll be here. But I think you're right. It is better if we keep things on a professional footing. I look forward to hearing about Luciana's progress a week on Saturday.'

And then he was gone.

Luis walked quickly away.

A week on Saturday. That was, what? Ten days? Eleven?

Eleven days to get his head together before he saw her again. To bury himself in work and make himself remember exactly why he had made this punishing, inhuman promise to Rico. And to wipe the memory of her extraordinary, erotic feet from his mind.

Or if that didn't work, to drink himself into oblivion.

CHAPTER TEN

THE touch on her face was as light as the caress of a butterfly's wing, but Emily couldn't suppress the shiver that rippled through her.

For the past eleven days she had been looking forward to this, the excitement mounting as the days went by. And now, finally, it was Saturday and every inch of her body was tingling, trembling with nerves and anticipation, so that just sitting still while the girl did her make-up was a major challenge.

It was the excitement of going to the ballet again, after all this time, she told herself. It had been more than six months since she'd last been to Covent Garden, just before Christmas when she and her mother made their usual trip to London for shopping and *The Nutcracker*—a tradition they'd followed since she was a child.

That seemed like a lifetime ago now.

Her eyes sprang open. The face that looked back at her, reflected from every angle by the triple mirror on the dressing table, was almost unrecognizable. Leaning forward she gave a little squeak of surprise and pleasure, batting her lashes and admiring the smoky-eyed effect that Eloisa, the make-up girl, had created with eyeliner and shadow.

'Oh, you're so clever! I look—'

'Sexy.' Eloisa spoke hardly any English, but she said this word with huge assurance, making Emily wonder fleetingly about the circumstances under which she'd picked it up.

'I was going to say grown-up,' she said ruefully, but Eloisa merely shrugged blankly and brandished a lipstick, making any further comment impossible.

Tipping her face up, Emily closed her eyes, and felt the butterflies rise up in her stomach once again as she parted her lips, and the darkness behind her lids was suddenly filled with images and memories. She almost gasped out loud as she felt the stroke of the brush against her quivering mouth, moving firmly, expertly over her lips…

'OK. *Pronto.*'

Eloisa's matter-of-fact voice brought Emily firmly back to reality and she opened her eyes, blinking guiltily and pressing her tingling lips together. Getting to her feet and going over to the full-length mirror she smoothed down the wine-red silk dress and raised a hand tentatively to touch the diamond comb that held her piled-up hair in place.

Gone was the wan, wide-eyed waif that Luis had brought with him to Santosa and in her place was a sophisticated dark-haired temptress. Thanks to the skill of the palace chef she had filled out, losing her previous gauntness so that her collarbones no longer stood out like coat hangers, and her pale breasts swelled slightly above the tight bodice of the red dress.

Standing behind her Eloisa sighed. *'Bonita, senhora. Príncipe Luis e muito afortunado.'*

Prince Luis.

Emily couldn't be sure what the rest of the sentence meant, but those two words leaped out at her as if they'd been accompanied by a foot-high sign.

'You go to the ballet?' Eloisa asked now, briskly stowing her brushes and pencils and pots of powder back into an industrial-size silver tool box.

'Yes.' Emily reached for the crisp voile wrap that matched her dress. The ballet. That's what she should be thinking of, focusing on. The ballet that she'd been looking forward to.

'Ahh…fabuloso.' Eloisa replied enviously. *'Qual balé?'*

Which ballet? Emily understood the question and opened her mouth to answer. And realised she couldn't for the life of her remember.

Sitting at the desk in his private suite of rooms Luis tried to focus on the charity report in front of him, and not on the whisky decanter he could see from the corner of his eye.

He could really do with a drink. It had been a draining day, one of many in an exhausting, cheerless and seemingly endless week when he had visited his father numerous times—publicly, to appease Josefina—made several statements to the press, which had varied from the simply anodyne to the blatantly untruthful, and begun to look properly into the huge and horrifying implications of what would happen when the King inevitably died.

The night at the Purple Parrot seemed like a very long time ago indeed.

Sighing he forced his mind back onto the report, glancing once again at the name of the charity printed at the top of the page. *The Santosan Preservation Trust*, it said in gold embossed letters. *Keeping Our Heritage Safe for the Future.*

Luis grimaced. He was trying to go through the charities of which King Marcos Fernando was patron and decide which ones he would continue to support personally, but it was a massive undertaking. And one that carried a very real risk of death by boredom. *We undertake to protect Santosa from the corrosive effects of the modern world,* he read wearily, *and preserve the values, traditions and environment which our ancestors worked so hard to establish.*

Luis sighed deeply. There were few things more depressing than the thought of Santosa being locked for ever in some suffocating bubble, cut off from reality and the rest of the world, but a quick look at the names on the Santosan Preservation Trust's board of governors—most of which made up the current government cabinet—told him that cutting royal ties with this particular charity might not be a popular decision. He put the paper on the growing pile of keepers and checked his watch.

She was exactly six minutes late. But since he'd practically been counting the hours until he would see her for the past eleven days, six minutes hardly mattered. *Deus,* it was ridiculous. He was like some hormonally unbalanced teenager. Impatiently he picked up the next report in the pile and opened it, hoping it was going to be something interesting enough to take his mind off the pull of desire low down in the pit of his stomach that had been with him almost constantly for more than a week.

It just confirmed how shallow and reprehensible he was, he thought bitterly. All the time he'd been sitting at his dying father's bedside, or going through the complicated practical and constitutional issues associated with the king's failing health and his own accession to the throne, all he could think about was Emily Balfour's mouth, her slender, supple body, glistening with water from the bath, her feet….

Deus, her feet…

He gritted his teeth and frowned. The problem was he wasn't used to wanting something—or someone—and not being able to have it. Since his mother had died his life had been about sublimating real emotions for sexual satisfaction, about instant gratification and taking what he wanted, when he wanted it, and the combination of his looks and his title had ensured no woman ever refused him.

Until he'd met Emily Balfour. Until he'd kissed her beneath the cherry blossom and she'd pulled away, and he had seen the fear in her wide blue eyes and realised what he had become.

There was a discreet knock at the door, and the duty footman appeared. 'Senhora Balfour, Your Highness.'

She was wearing red. At first that was all Luis was aware of, other than that she was the most extraordinarily beautiful girl he had ever seen.

Woman, not girl, he corrected himself mentally, as his gaze moved slowly over her. The dress had a close-fitting bodice that showed off the narrowness of her frame and her small, perfect breasts, while the billowing full skirt that fell to just above her ankles emphasized her hips. And, he noticed with a pang, made it possible to see her feet.

Without realising it he had got up, and suddenly he was aware that he was standing by the desk, the pen still in his hand, staring at her. He threw the pen down and ran a finger round the collar of his evening shirt as he went towards her.

'Sorry,' he said curtly, leaning down to give her a perfunctory kiss on each cheek. 'I'm just catching up on some paperwork. I was miles away.'

He pulled away from her quickly, as if she were red hot. Which she was, he thought darkly. Dangerously so, in every sense.

She lowered her eyes with a sweep of impossibly long black lashes, and Luis felt a moment of relief to be shielded from that direct blue gaze. 'I'm sorry—if you're busy I can always wait outside until you're ready…?'

'No.' The word came out as an autocratic bark. *Deus*, Josefina would be thrilled at such uncharacteristic regality. 'That won't be necessary. Would you like a drink before we go?'

She looked up at him uncertainly. 'Are you having one?'

'I can't.' No matter how much he needed one. He nodded in the direction of one of the rows of windows which looked out over the circular sweep of lawn beyond the formal garden. The helicopter waited there, the setting sun glinting on the royal crest on the side. 'I'm flying.'

Her eyes widened. 'We're going in that? Alone?'

'Yes. It's the quickest way to travel to the mainland. Not as comfortable as the jet, of course, but more direct. Is that a problem?'

'No…no, of course not,' she stammered, but not before he had seen the expression of alarm flicker across her face and knew that she was thinking of Rico.

'Good,' he said blandly, picking up his mobile phone and

walking towards the door. He had been about to reassure her that it was quite safe, but that was an untruth too far. 'Shall we go, then?'

The diaphanous wrap she wore brushed against the back of his hand as she walked past him through the door, and he caught a fleeting breath of the delicate scent of her skin. 'You look beautiful, by the way.'

That much at least was true.

Being a Cordoba is about saying the correct thing, not the honest thing. Wasn't that what he'd said that night at the restaurant? *That's the deal and you can't change it.*

No, well, he could at least have made it sound a little bit like he meant it when he said she looked beautiful.

Emily's heels sank into the soft earth as she walked across the lawn to the waiting helicopter, hampering her efforts to keep pace with Luis's swift stride. Not that she really felt like it now. She'd been looking forward to this evening for so long, and the moment she'd seen him of course she knew there was no point in trying to convince herself that her excitement had much to do with the ballet.

It was him.

The truly humiliating thing was he'd been right all along. She was the immature, inexperienced kid he had accused her of being, and she had a whopping great, embarrassing school-girl crush on him.

Ahead of her one of the uniformed personnel standing by the helicopter pulled open the door and Luis jumped lithely up into the cockpit, then turned round to hold out a hand to her. Emily faltered, unwilling to take it, unable to look at him in case he saw the longing in her eyes.

'Thanks but it's fine. I can manage,' she muttered, gathering her skirt up and climbing inelegantly in beside him. Not that he noticed. Already he had turned away from her and was un-hooking the headset that was suspended above the control panel, flicking switches, checking dials and signalling to the crew circling around them on the ground.

'Put on your headset—we're ready for take-off.'

Emily did as she was told, relieved at least that, both wearing headsets, they would be spared the need to make polite conversation. Not that Luis, given his obvious preoccupation, would have bothered anyway.

With a roar the rotor blades started up and the ground swayed and receded beneath them as they rose vertically into the sky.

It was a beautiful evening. Within moments they were suspended in a soft, forget-me-not blue sky with the palace spread out below them like some elaborate doll's house belonging to a spoiled child. It was an incredible view, but Emily found herself more preoccupied with the sight of Luis's strong, golden hands on the helicopter's cyclic. The cockpit was small enough for her shoulder to be almost touching his, and the whole of the side of her body nearest him tingled and buzzed, as if tiny magnets beneath her skin were pulling her towards him.

It was going to be an uncomfortable journey.

They had left the palace behind now and were heading over the trees and flat, rolling grassland of the royal estate out towards the sea which glittered ahead of them, and the realization that she was cut off from the rest of the world with him sent a spasm of panicky longing ricocheting through her.

'OK?'

She jumped as his voice came through her headset, caressing her ear with an intimacy that made her shiver. Glancing across at him she felt her stomach constrict. He was wearing the same aviator sunglasses he'd worn the day he'd kissed her on the tarmac at the airport, and combined with the exquisitely tailored dinner suit and black tie, the effect was nothing short of devastating.

'Fine,' she murmured faintly, forcing herself to look away. 'Just admiring the scenery. What's that down there?'

Luis followed her gaze to the slate-roofed building nestling in the trees beneath them. *'La Guarita,'* he said in husky Portuguese, and Emily felt the hairs rise on the back of her neck. 'It was built by one of my more extravagant ancestors to be used as a hunting lodge.'

Emily nodded gravely. It could have been the local supermarket for all she cared, but the sensation of his voice in her ear was exquisite and she didn't want it to stop. 'A hunting lodge? It's not very rustic. Tell me more about this ancestor of yours.'

Luis threw her a twisted smile. 'On one condition. That afterwards you tell me the plot of this ballet we're going to see.'

'Done.'

A fat lot of good that had been, Luis thought savagely, staring at the stage in a welter of boredom a couple of hours later. Emily had done her best, but try as he might he just couldn't reconcile the story she had told him about some peasant girl who had fallen in love—with a nobleman, or a huntsman?—with the ridiculous leaping and writhing that was happening on stage.

He slumped back in his seat and rubbed a hand over his eyes. Mind you, if he'd actually been listening properly to what she was saying rather than just enjoying the sweetness of her voice in his ear he might have understood a whole lot more. But he was finding that it was impossible to concentrate on anything much when she was around, and that was seriously beginning to bother him.

From the moment they'd stepped out of the car that had brought them from the helipad he had sensed the tautness in her body, and once again he was reminded of a racehorse—alert and quivering with nerves, but strong and true and courageous beneath the delicate exterior. Walking beside him up the wide marble steps to the opera house she had allowed him to take her arm, but he could feel the distance she placed between them like an invisible force field. At least the photographers were unaware of it as they snapped excitedly away. Finally it seemed Josefina would get what she wanted.

If only, he thought with cutting self-mockery, there was a chance that he would too.

His gaze shifted back to where she was sitting, leaning forward in her seat, her hands gripping the edge of the box as she looked down over the stage. There was nothing overtly sexy about the scarlet dress she wore—except perhaps the colour—but on her even the demurely high back that showed only a narrow crescent of creamy skin on her shoulders seemed to be excruciatingly provocative. It took all his willpower just to stop himself from reaching out and touching the single curl that spiralled down from the nape of her neck.

Despairingly he pulled his mobile phone from the pocket of his jacket and glared down at the screen. The next hour was going to be hell anyway, so he might as well pile on the torture and get through some emails as well. Boredom beat frustrated lust any day.

The huge full moon cast a soft luminescence over the stage. Emily kept her eyes fixed unblinkingly on it as the audience below rose from their red velvet seats. It had been a breathtaking, heartbreaking performance and the tumult of applause went on and on.

Only she sat frozen and still.

On the stage the dancers swept forward again to bow to the enchanted audience, the white dresses of the ballerinas billowing out as they made their deep, graceful curtsies, their faces uniformly composed in spite of the wrenching sadness of the dance they had just finished. For as long as she could remember Emily had wanted only to be like them—flawless and doll-like in white tulle and satin shoes. For years she had devoted her life to training her body, rigidly controlling and disciplining it to achieve that cool, remote perfection.

And she had. Only to realise—too late—that she'd missed the point all along. Being a dancer wasn't just about precision or perfection or lucky shoes.

It was about emotion.

And that was something she'd deliberately, ruthlessly, shut out since the day her mother was diagnosed with terminal cancer. It was how she had got through Mia's arrival and the realization that her father had betrayed and lied to them all. It was what had enabled her to calmly and quietly walk away from Balfour the day after her mother's funeral.

But it was also what had taken away her ability to dance.

She stumbled to her feet. Groping behind her for her wrap she caught sight of Luis, and realised that she wasn't the only one in the audience not clapping. Lounging back in his seat, he had his mobile phone in his hand and was tapping away at it. In the greenish light of the screen his face was a mask of boredom.

He looked up. She was caught in the dark vortex of his gaze, and in that moment she understood that the terrifying, uncontrollable emotions she had spent the past six exhausting months trying to run away from she hadn't escaped at all, because they were inside her all along.

Slowly he unfolded his long, lithe body from the seat and stood in front of her, his face expressionless. At some point during the performance he had surreptitiously undone his top button and his black silk tie, which now hung loosely around his neck. He looked frighteningly beautiful.

'Finally.' His lips twitched into a crooked smile. 'I thought it would never end. You don't look like you enjoyed it much either.'

'I loved it,' she said, her voice hollow and fierce.

'Really?' His arched brows rose in surprise. 'Well, that's lucky, I suppose, because I have a proposition for you.' He reached down and picked up her wrap, which was trailing over the back of the chair, and in one practised movement settled it lightly over her shoulders, his fingers brushing her skin for the merest fraction of a second.

Emily steeled herself against the shuddering awareness that gripped her, but then he was taking her hands and drawing her gently backwards so they were concealed behind the heavy velvet curtain that hung down at the side of the royal box and she felt herself go rigid with panic.

'Wh-what are you doing?' Her voice came out as a frozen whisper, and he dropped her hands immediately, his face curiously blank.

'Relax,' he said wearily, 'I'm not trying to ravish you behind the curtains, but in case you hadn't noticed the entire audience have now shifted their attention from the stage to us.'

Emily darted a glance over her shoulder. Her breathing was shallow and uneven. Below them the lights had gone up and the hum of conversation had resumed as people put back their opera glasses and gathered their evening bags. Several of them still had their faces turned up towards the royal box. Frowning, she turned back to Luis.

'Please—can we go now?'

'Wait.' His face was shadowed by the fall of the curtain, but she could see the dull gleam of his eyes and the flicker of a muscle in his cheek. 'I have something to ask you first.'

The shadows closed in on her a little and she took a small, gasping breath.

'It's my father's Silver Jubilee this year and there's going to be some kind of event to mark it,' he said dully. 'The Brazilian National Ballet are scheduled to perform there. We'd like you and Luciana to dance with them.'

She opened her mouth to laugh at the irony, but instead it came out as a sob. She shook her head, biting down on her bottom lip as her fragile shell of control threatened to crack.

'Impossible,' she said in a tight, cold voice. 'I'm afraid I couldn't. Now please, can we just go?'

Two men in suits had appeared at the doorway to the box, their ubiquitous headsets clearly marking them out as palace bodyguards. Luis seemed to hesitate for a moment, his face as cool and blank as marble, but then he gave a curt nod and the security men opened the door and went ahead of them, down the dimly lit VIP staircase that led directly to the main foyer.

Emily was glad of the gloom. Surreptitiously she sniffed and pressed the palms of her hands to her cheeks, desperately trying to stem the tears that had started to slide down her face in a silent stream and keep herself from being sucked down into despair.

The door at the foot of the stairs opened, letting in a blast of noise from the hallway beyond and the clear evening light. Emily blinked, instinctively wanting to hide her tear-stained face, but it was too late. The guards stood aside, holding the door open and motioning them to go through, to the car that waited at the foot of the steps outside.

Luis glanced down at her and in that split second she saw a flare of some unfathomable emotion in the depths of his eyes. His reactions were as swift and devastating as lightning. Instantly his arm was around her shoulders, sheltering her against the protective wall of his body as he pulled her forwards. He raised his other hand to wave to the crowd, but Emily understood that it was also shielding her from the glittering camera flashes and the glare of onlookers.

As they went out into the still-warm evening and down the steps she kept her body rigid, every atom of her being resisting the urge to melt against him. But then his grip on her relaxed as they approached the waiting car and an arrow of desolation shot through her. She raised her head just at she same moment he looked down at her.

Afterwards she couldn't have said how it happened, or who made the first move. All she knew was that one moment he was reaching out to open the door of the car for her and the next he had taken her upturned face between his strong hands and their mouths had come together in a hard, helpless kiss.

It lasted only seconds. And then she was in the car and he was beside her and they were pulling away from the screaming, ecstatic crowd.

CHAPTER ELEVEN

IT WAS a heartbreakingly beautiful evening. As they flew back to Santosa the sun was setting over the sea, streaking the clear turquoise water with ribbons of rose and gold, and turning the white sand of the many beaches fringing the islands of the archipelago to pink sherbet.

Was this how it was for Rico, flying home that night? Luis wondered bleakly. It was oddly comforting to think that his last moments on earth had been like this—a foretaste of the paradise in which he was assured a place.

Unlike Luis.

Beside him Emily sat, taut and silent. They had barely spoken since they left the opera house, and although he had tried to say 'sorry' she had batted his apologies straight back in a way that told him this time things were different. She seemed angry with him, which he couldn't blame her for in the slightest, but hell, he thought savagely, she couldn't be more angry than he was with himself.

He glanced across at her. The setting sun gilded her perfect profile, sprinkling gold dust on her long, luxuriant lashes, her delicate slightly upturned nose, and he had to crush another debilitating spasm of want. *Deus*, he raged silently, staring out into the apricot heavens, wasn't it punishment enough that he'd given it all up, without this cruel temptation, this constant, tantalising reminder of the pleasures that he'd forsworn?

'I'm sorry.'

Her subdued voice came through his headset. Luis felt his whole body tense and he smiled grimly.

'I think that's my line,' he drawled. 'What are *you* sorry for?'

She was very still, her head bent. 'For being so ungrateful earlier. For turning down what was a very…generous offer.'

The dancing. She was talking about the dancing, he realised. Oddly enough he'd forgotten all about that, but suddenly his curiosity was aroused. Which made a change from other, baser parts of him. 'Good point,' he said tersely. 'So why did you turn it down? I thought you'd be pleased.'

Beneath them the shadow of the helicopter skimmed serenely over the silken sea, giving absolutely no indication of the electrifying tension that crackled inside the small space inside.

'Because it's out of the question. I just…can't.'

'Can't, or won't?' Such was his awareness of her body beside him that he felt her startle at the harshness of his tone, but he didn't seem to be able to soften it. 'Naturally a suggestion like that wasn't made without a bit of preliminary research, and according to the principal of your school you were the most talented dancer of your year.'

'*Was,*' she said bitterly. 'Past tense.'

They were flying over a long stretch of innocuous-looking white sand, edged on one side by a clear sea that in the fiery light of the dying sun looked like pink champagne. It was here that the wreckage of Rico's helicopter had been found, washed up at the base of the steep cliffs which cast their jagged shadows over the beach. Flying towards them Luis kept his voice carefully flat. 'What changed?'

'I did.' She laughed, and the headset magnified the despair in it. 'You were right—I was just a kid then, a silly, naive little girl. And then I grew up and the magic just…went. Like when you stop believing in fairy tales.' Her head was turned away from him, but in her lap he could see that her hands were twisted together in a tight knot of anguish, almost as if she were trying to hold on to herself. 'I can do the steps,' she went on, in a low, toneless voice. 'Go through the motions, and I can do it so *perfectly* that sometimes I can almost convince myself I might still be a dancer. But tonight…' she faltered. 'Tonight I realised how far from the truth that is. There's no passion there. I just can't feel it.'

Luis remembered what Oscar had said that night on the telephone. *She doesn't do anything in half-measures. Never has. Whatever she does she does passionately, with her whole heart and soul.*

The cliffs were right in front of them now and suddenly from the benevolent golden sunshine of evening they plunged into cool gloom that only served to tighten the atmosphere in the confined space. Sharply Luis brought the helicopter upwards, and as he did so his arm brushed against hers. She gave a muffled cry and jerked away, as if he had burnt her.

It was like the first crack of thunder in a storm that had been brewing for hours. Swearing under his breath Luis steadied the helicopter and looked across at her, his heartbeat echoing loudly in his own ears.

'Don't tell me you don't feel it,' he said through gritted teeth. 'Don't tell me you're not passionate because—'

'I'm *scared*!'

The words seemed to be torn from somewhere inside her. Luis flinched, everything in him tensing as if against a blow. Adrenaline coursed through him so that it took all his skill and self-control to keep the helicopter flying straight. It was what he'd always known, since the night that he'd first met her. She'd seen through him, to the contemptible person beneath the veneer. 'Of me?' he said in a voice that dripped despair and self-disgust. '*Deus*, Emily—'

'No. *No.*' Emily splayed her hands out on her knees, staring down at them and speaking deliberately and carefully. She was aware of her heart beating, very hard, as if it was trying to break free of the restraints of the tight, red silk.

'Not of you. Of *me*.' She broke off with a ragged, self-mocking laugh. 'There. That's the reason I can't do it. Because I'm scared of letting go. I'm *scared* of all the feelings inside me spilling out and…and…I don't know, sucking me down, overwhelming me…'

The words faded in the tense, buzzing silence. Oh, God, what had she said? She didn't dare look across at Luis, scared to see the mockery and contempt on his beautiful, cruel face. The helicopter was coming lower, she realised with a stab of despair. They were back at the palace and in a moment men in uniforms with blank faces would be opening the doors, forcing her out into the real world again. She would go back to her lavish, lonely suite and the silence and the emptiness, and he would walk away, thinking she was insane.

She closed her eyes, squeezing them tight like she used to do when she was a child and believed that you could get anything by wishing hard enough. They were descending quickly, and she waited for the slight thud of solid ground beneath them before she opened her eyes.

She blinked, expecting to see the wide lawn and the palace beyond, but here it was dark. Secret. She blinked again, looking round in disbelief. They were in a clearing, surrounded by trees.

'Wh-where—? What—?'

Slowly Luis pulled off his headset and ran a hand through his hair. 'Sorry,' he said in a voice like broken glass. 'I can't fly like this. I'm not safe. Security will come over soon. You can fly back with them.'

'No.'

He turned to look at her. His face—his high-cheekboned face with its generous, sensual mouth—was set hard, as if he was silently enduring some private torment, but those narrow, golden eyes were as dark as treacle, burning with an emotion that made her gasp.

'I don't want to be safe,' she whispered.

She was shaking. Trembling with fear and excitement and

wild, urgent need. They weren't touching at all, but their eyes were locked together.

'Emily, do you know what you're saying—?'

'Yes,' she said, so quietly it was little more than a shivering breath. 'Oh, yes.'

The forest was deep and dark, and as Luis pulled her through the trees some ragged birds rose, flapping and shrieking into the faded sky. Emily jumped, her footsteps faltering, so that Luis turned back to look at her. In the velvet twilight his expression was tortured.

'Do you want to go back?'

'*No.*'

It was a low, primal moan. Hearing it seemed to release some instinct in him that he was trying to suppress and he stopped and took her face between his hands, crashing his mouth down on hers and kissing her as if he almost wanted to devour her. As his mouth crushed her lips and moved across her jaw, her throat, Emily felt her shaking legs buckle and collapsed against the trunk of a massive tree, surrendering to the waves of ecstasy that were battering her.

Suddenly Luis pulled away, and cold dread gripped her.

'Don't stop…please, Luis…'

'*Christo*, I have to,' he ground out through gritted teeth. 'Otherwise I won't be able to. In a few minutes the sky up there is going to be swarming with helicopters looking for us, and I wouldn't like to corrupt the innocence of the security team by letting them see me making love to you on the forest floor.'

Emily laughed, but it came out as a desperate sob of need. Luis took her face in his hands again, stroking his thumbs across her cheeks, gazing into her eyes with a scorching intensity that made her feel like her whole body was on fire. 'Are you sure this is what you want?'

Incoherent, frantic with longing, Emily could only nod, but the expression in her eyes must have told him all he needed to know because the next moment he was taking her hand. With a muffled curse that sounded like a plea for forgiveness he was pulling her onwards again so that she had to gather up her scarlet silk skirts and run to keep up. Slipping through the gloom beneath the trees she felt like Red Riding Hood, all grown up and not afraid of the wolf any more

Ahead of them a high wall reared up, blocking out the remainder of the dying light. Luis headed for a steel gate set into it, and dropped Emily's hand long enough to press his finger onto a small electronic pad and then key in a number. A second later the gate swung heavily open.

'It's the house we saw from the helicopter,' Emily murmured, as Luis seized her hand again and led her towards a low stone house with a steeply sloping gabled roof that made it look exactly like a picture from a child's storybook.

At the door Luis went through the same process with the fingerprint and the security number. Emily's heart was beating so hard it shook her entire body, sending jets of adrenaline through her with every racking thud. Her skin felt hypersensitive, so that the feel of his hand grazing the top of her bare arm as she went through the door he held open for her made her shiver and suck in a breath.

She jumped as the door closed behind them.

The large, open-plan room smelled of wood smoke and was full of dusk and shadows. Emily stood in its centre, unable to look around her or take anything in apart from Luis. After shutting the door he leaned back against it and for endless minutes neither of them moved. His dark gaze seared into her through the twilight, pinioning her to the spot in an agony of helpless longing. A pulse throbbed insistently at the apex of her thighs, each beat increasing the quivering, tingling tension. She was aware of a wetness inside her that both thrilled and horrified her.

'I'm scared.'

The whispered words had left her lips before she could stop

them, and the instant she had spoken she pressed her teeth into her bottom lip, wishing she could take them back. Slowly Luis levered himself away from the door and came towards her, his eyes never leaving hers.

'You don't have to be scared.' Standing in front of her he seemed hugely tall, impossibly broad shouldered and strong. Head tipped slightly back, he took her hands in his and held them, hard. 'You can stop all this now…any time you want.'

Wide-eyed, trembling, she looked up at him. '*No. I want this. So much.* But…' She swallowed.

His grip on her hands tightened. 'But what?'

'I'm scared because I don't know what to do. What if I can't…? What if I'm no good—?'

With a moan he let go of her hands and stepped back, clenching his fists for a moment before pushing his fingers through his hair. '*Deus*, Emily. It's all I can do to control myself right now, standing here in front of you in that dress.'

'But you've had so many women. Beautiful women. Women who know how to p-pl-pleasure a man…what to do to t-turn you on.'

'That's all in the past,' he said bleakly. 'This is about now. About you, and you don't have to *do* anything. You turn me on so much just by the way you move, the way you talk—*Christo*, just the way you breathe…'

Without knowing what she was doing Emily had brought her hands up to her mouth, pressing her fingers against her lips to silence the whimpers of longing that threatened to escape her as his rough, raw voice vibrated through her. Very gently now he took hold of her wrists and pulled her hands down, drawing her forward towards the stairs

'Just you. As you are. No technicalities. No precise, practised steps, remember?'

The stairs led straight up into a single, large room under the eaves of the house. A window at one end looked straight out over the forest, and above the tops of the trees Emily could see the silver glimmer of a crescent moon in the blue velvet sky. She took a step towards it, expelling a shaky breath.

'Close your eyes.'

Luis was standing behind her. She did as she was told, and a moment later felt his hand on her waist, while he very gently lifted her arm, trailing his fingers lingeringly along the sensitive skin on its underside. It was like a movement from the ballet—part of the *grand adage*, the slow and seductive courtship between the dancers. She felt her spine flexing, her pelvis tilting back towards him, her body coming to life in his hands.

Slowly, inch by inch, his fingers stroked their path of bliss over her shoulder and along the curve of her neck until finally they reached the zip fastening of her dress. Unhurriedly they lingered there, caressing a curl of hair that had escaped from its twist. She could feel his breath, warm on her neck, could feel the heat spreading inside her, the dampness seeping down between her trembling thighs, and she knew that she had to hold herself very still, very rigid, to ride the waves of deranging ecstasy that were swelling within her.

Her eyes were still tightly shut, the darkness magnifying every touch, every sensation. It was getting harder to stop the shivers of pleasure that were building inside of her, and as she felt him begin to ease the zip of her dress down she stiffened with the effort, biting down, hard, on her lip to keep herself from crying out.

He stopped. Her eyes flew open as, horrified, she thought he had had second thoughts, decided after all that she wasn't sexy or exciting or seductive enough. But then she felt his mouth brush her nape, his breath caressing her, his tongue tracing silken circles around the vertebra at the base of her neck.

This time she couldn't hold back the deep shudder of desire. His hands came up to grip her shoulders, holding her steady as she tipped back her head and gave a gasp of pleasure and anguish.

'It's OK…' he whispered hoarsely. 'It's OK to let go…'

'*I can't…*'

'You can…*querida*, you can whenever you want to.'

He had eased the zip of her dress the rest of the way down now, right to her waist. Emily sucked her stomach in, her whole body tensing as his big, skilled, steady hands moved over her back, stroking the rigid angles of her shoulder blades, his thumbs finding the hollows above her hips as his fingers slipped beneath the gaping satin bodice to gently brush her waist. Emily crossed her arms over her chest, holding the dress against her bare breasts as her head fell heavily forward, her spine arching helplessly.

'I want to see you.'

Her head snapped up and a protest sprang to her lips, but it was useless—Luis was already turning her around to face him. The dying light from the window behind her turned his skin to dull gold, and the reflection of the moon shone in eyes which were dark, fathomless pools.

Her arms were still locked across her chest. She half expected him to peel them away, but he made no move to do so. Instead he reached out and touched her mouth lightly with his fingertips.

'You're exquisite,' he said simply.

And that one butterfly touch, combined with the intensity of his moon-drenched gaze, broke through the bonds which held her back. With his fingers still against her mouth she parted her lips, exhaling a ragged, needy breath and in an instant she was crushed against him as he kissed her with a wildness and an urgency that made everything that had come before seem like a childish game.

It was as if she had been locked in some dark, cramped place and he had released her. Just as he had opened the door to this secret house of shadows with one touch of his fingertip, so had he magically unlocked a secret, joyful part of her that wasn't afraid and didn't care about being perfect. There was nothing disciplined in the wantonness with which she kissed him back—her tongue tangling with his, her lips exploring, tasting, sucking, tearing—and nothing controlled in the way her shaking fingers fumbled with the buttons of his shirt, desperate to touch his warm skin.

His hands were in her hair, working with considerably more finesse at the diamond comb and the pins which held it up, swiftly and expertly dispatching them until the elegant pleat uncoiled and fell about her shoulders. Pulling back from her he held her at arm's length for a moment, giving a subdued moan as he raked his fingers through it, tousling it out of its sleekness. She had forgotten to hold the top of her dress up, and it fell down over her shoulders, half exposing her breasts.

'I think it's time to take this off,' he said roughly, pushing it down completely and sliding it over her hips so it settled on the floor in a crimson pool.

She heard him breathe in, felt him recoil slightly, his whole body tensing as she stepped out of it. For a moment all her doubts returned, but as she glanced anxiously up at his face she saw that it was desire he was struggling to control, and a second later he had scooped her up into his arms and was carrying her across to the wide bed at the other end of the room.

The sheets were cool beneath her back and she spread herself across them. He bent over her, and she caught the dark gleam of his eyes, the clean musk scent of his skin as he lowered his head and took her tight nipple in his mouth. Ten thousand volts of bliss shot through her and she cried out, jerking convulsively as his hands held her steady, but he didn't stop. Inch by quivering inch he covered her body with a thoroughness that felt like reverence, until Emily was floating, spaced out, incandescent.

She wasn't aware of him taking off the rest of his clothes, but as she felt the hard warmth of his flesh against hers she registered his nakedness. For a second he pulled away from her, and she glimpsed the astonishing, magnificence of his erection as he deftly rolled on a condom, and she felt she was teetering on the edge of some dizzying precipice she hadn't even known was there. Her legs twined helplessly around him, her supple body moulding against him as she opened herself up to his kisses. Dimly she was aware that he was holding her waist, lifting her on top of him so she was astride his hips, and she wasn't sure whether the throbbing, tightness she could feel beneath her was her own body or his. Instinctively she raised herself up on her knees, arching backwards, sweeping her hair off her hot damp neck as she tilted her hips, hungry for him.

'I want…more…. All of you…'

In one fluid movement he had levered himself up and was holding her against him, taking her face between his hands, kissing her fiercely before rolling her over onto the bed and towering above her. His perfect face was cool and remote, his expression almost abstracted as with infinite tenderness he entered her.

She had expected it to hurt, had stiffened momentarily in anticipation, but there was nothing but an incredible feeling of relief—relief so strong she could have wept with it. But already another sensation was overtaking her, one so powerful and compelling that it made everything else slide out of focus—a sort of exquisite sweetness that gripped her body so tightly that it felt almost like pain.

She opened her eyes, gazing up at him in panic, as the fear of being overwhelmed…out of control came back. And then for a split second she saw the expression in his eyes, the intensity of his desire, before his eyelids flickered and closed and she knew that this strong, fearless man was surrendering too. His powerful body tensed, the hard muscles of his back bunching beneath her hands as he thrust inside her again.

It was too late. She couldn't hold on, couldn't hold herself together any more, and she was falling, shattering, dissolving…

Except he was there, anchoring her and holding her safe, rocking her, and murmuring into her hair as the spasms of aching bliss gripped her body and then went on shuddering through her like the aftershocks of a massive earthquake.

Lying in the ruins she knew that nothing would ever look the same again.

* * *

'I never dreamed I could feel like that.'

Emily's head was on his chest, her fingers idly caressing his upper arm. Looking up into the high, sloping eaves, just as he had done so many times over the years when he'd brought women here, Luis smiled bleakly.

'Neither did I.'

She raised herself up on her elbows, looking down into his face with a slight frown. It was almost completely dark outside now, but her blue eyes glowed with a luminescence that came from within her.

'Was it OK?'

Was it OK. He didn't know what to say. OK didn't really begin to describe what had happened back there.

'It was more than OK.'

'I'm sorry that I didn't do all the things for you that you did for me…' Her blue eyes were suddenly hidden by a downward sweep of her lashes.

'It was just as well you didn't. I wouldn't have lasted two minutes if you had.' Watching her gradually let go, give herself up, lose control, had been the most intensely erotic experience of his life, but for that very reason it had also been one of the most challenging. To rein himself back and control his own devouring lust after so long had been agonising and exhausting and exhilarating…and ultimately profoundly satisfying. It made him realise that up until now he hadn't known the meaning of making love. What he had been doing before with that long procession of anonymous women was like picking out a nursery rhyme tune with one finger on the piano. Joining dots. Colouring in a crude drawing with crayons. This had been a concert-standard, full rendition of *Beethoven's Ninth*, a masterpiece in oils.

'Next time,' she said softly, her hand moving downwards.

From outside he could hear the drone of a helicopter. He got up abruptly, swearing in Portuguese as he reached for the clothes he had thrown on the floor.

'We need to get dressed.'

'Luis—'

'We don't have long before the royal security force smashes its way in here to see if we've been kidnapped by terrorists, so please…' He picked up her dress and went over to the bed with it, trying not to breathe in the scent of her that clung to the red silk because he knew it would weaken his resolve.

Clutching the sheet to her she sat up and took it from him, her eyes huge with terrible emotion—dread, anguish, hurt.

'You're trying to tell me there won't be a next time, aren't you? This is it—'

He stopped in the middle of buttoning up his shirt and spun round to face her. '*Deus*, Emily, that's not what I want.' His hands, dropping to his sides, curled reflexively into fists. 'But you deserve much more than I can give you.'

'I'm not a child, Luis.' She got to her feet, still holding the dress bundled up in her arms. Against the darkness of her hair and the scarlet silk her face was very white. 'Not any more. I don't want some neat and perfect fairy-tale happy ending. I want this.' She came towards him, her strong bare feet making no sound on the wooden boards, her eyes as clear and unclouded as a summer sky. 'It's like all the things I've never quite understood suddenly make sense now, and after years of controlling and disciplining my body and forcing it to be perfect I finally know what it's really for.'

She put her hand flat against his bare chest, over his heart. His muscles instantly tensed against the violent longing that leapt within him.

'Meaningless sex?' He had meant it to sound sardonic, a mocking reference to that night back in the hotel in England, but the bitterness in his voice cut through the soft shadows between them like razor blades.

She didn't flinch. When she replied her voice was soft and thick, like velvet, and it wrapped around him. 'Yes, if you want to put it like that. Meaningless sex.'

Outside the staccato whirr of the helicopters was getting

louder. Luis looked towards the window, panic and despair welling within him.

Forgive me, Rico, he thought bleakly. *Forgive me, but understand this…I haven't broken my promise…*

Standing over Rico's coffin the night before the funeral he had made a vow to give up the casual meaningless sex with women whose names he barely knew.

And he had.

The thing that frightened him now was that this was something entirely different.

CHAPTER TWELVE

EMILY wrote to Oscar.

She began by writing *Dear Daddy*, because that was how she and her sisters had always addressed him, but something about the childish term sounded odd now. Swallowing her misgivings she plunged on.

> *I know from Luis that you won't be surprised by the address at the top of this page. He tells me that he has been in touch with you several times since I met him by chance in London. I'm grateful to him for that. At the time I thought I was managing everything perfectly well when actually I wasn't thinking straight about anything at all, and I didn't stop to think how worried you must have been.*

She stopped here, the nib of her pen poised above the velvety surface of the palace notepaper. That wasn't quite right either. She had realised how worried he would be, but the truth was she'd been too angry with him to care.

How selfish and childish that seemed now.

She continued, smiling a little as she wrote Luis's name.

> *I'm grateful to Luis for so much. Amongst other things, he has enabled me to see how badly I behaved towards you after Mia arrived. Looking back now I'm ashamed of how*

judgemental I was, and how immature and naive. I hope that you'll forgive me, and that Mia will too. I've written to her separately—is she still staying with you at Balfour?

Suddenly it struck her how long she'd been away. Not so very long in terms of weeks and months perhaps, but in terms of everything that had happened. When she'd left it had been winter, and her mother's presence had still filled the house. If she went back now would she find that Lillian's spirit, the gentle serenity she always brought to a place, would be gone too?

A tear fell onto the page and she quickly blotted it, starting to write again.

I'm here, as I'm sure you know, to teach ballet to Luis's niece, Luciana, whose parents were so tragically killed in a helicopter crash last year—I'm sure you remember. At first she didn't talk much at all—about that or anything else—but as I've got to know her better she's opened up a lot more, and I now think that one of the saddest things about what's happened is that she didn't really feel close to her parents or loved by them. It has made me realise how lucky I was to have you and Mum and to be so loved and protected. So much so that in some ways I was unprepared for the real world, like the princess in the tower in the fairy story you used to read to me when I was little. I suppose I never thought about what would happen when the time came—as it inevitably must—to leave that tower and go out into the big bad world, and it's been harder and more painful than I could have imagined. But it's also been...

Here she stopped again, not knowing how to convey on paper, to her father, the bittersweet rapture of the past few weeks. Sweet because Luis had freed her from the fears of losing control, of not being perfect, of being overwhelmed by the forbidden desires she had always known lay just below the surface. He had, ironically, brought all of these fears to fruition, but in doing so had shown her that she didn't have to be afraid or ashamed any more.

But the bitter edge came from knowing she couldn't touch him in the same way that he touched her. That while she had opened herself up to him completely, there was still a part of him that he kept hidden from her. Hidden and locked and barred.

With a sigh she looked back down at the page in front of her: *…wonderful*, she finished, lamely. Biting her lip she began to write more quickly, suddenly wanting to get the letter finished and in the post to Oscar.

> *I'm also dancing properly again—another thing for which I have Luis to thank. I am taking part in King Marcos Fernando's Silver Jubilee celebration, performing as a soloist with the Brazilian National Ballet. I'm doing a pas de deux from* Giselle, *and Luciana is doing a little dance from* The Nutcracker. *I was wondering if perhaps…*

She frowned, her usually neat handwriting beginning to slope.

> *…you might think about coming over to watch it? I know that the King is an old friend of yours from way back and I gather that he's not in the best of health so you shouldn't put off coming if you want to see him again…*

She looked at her watch. She had been longer than she'd thought and the car would be waiting to take her to Santosa's *Grande Teatro*. Moistening her lips with her tongue she plunged on, not wanting to think too hard about what she was writing in case she lost her nerve.

> *Of course, what I'm really saying is that* I *want to see you, so badly. I've missed you so very much.*

Hastily she finished, tears blurring her eyes as she signed off with her love and wrote the familiar address, just as she had done every Sunday night for all those years when she'd been away at ballet school. Then she scooped up the thick cream envelope, along with her bottle of water and towel for the rehearsal, and went down to leave it on the post table in the hall, before she could change her mind.

'I'm worried about you.'

Luis eyed his father cynically. 'Coming from a man in your condition, that *is* disturbing.'

King Marcos Fernando gave a snort of wheezing laughter that threatened to dislodge the oxygen tube beneath his nose. 'That's more like it,' he huffed, when he'd recovered enough breath to speak again. 'A spark of the old Luis. I haven't seen enough of that these past few months.'

'No, well it would hardly have been appropriate to be sitting here cracking jokes while you're—'

'On my deathbed? Why not? It might have taken my mind off things a bit. Far too much time to lie here and think. And worry. About you mainly.'

'You and the rest of the royal household,' Luis said levelly, looking out of the window of the private clinic onto a severely well-maintained garden filled with gaudy flowers. 'Tomás and Josefina are on tranquilisers at the thought of me taking the throne.'

'Well, it was a role you were never supposed to have.' Never the most tactful of men, illness and a sense of time running out had made King Marcos more blunt than ever. 'You're not made for it like Rico was. It won't be easy for you like it would have been for him.'

'Thanks a lot.'

The king ignored the undisguised sarcasm in his second son's tone. 'It's an observation, not a criticism. Anyway,' he said shortly, resting a blue-veined hand on a pile of newspapers on the table over the bed. 'You seem to be doing everything right these days—taking an interest in the charities, sounding suitably concerned about your decrepit old father, managing to keep your sexual adventuring out of the papers…' He looked across at Luis shrewdly. 'Where's the catch?'

Luis kept his tone and expression deliberately blank. 'What do you mean?'

His father shifted in the bed, wincing momentarily as he knocked the tube that was dispensing colourless fluid into the back of his hand. 'There's always a catch with you,' he said breathlessly. 'When you were at school I worried most about you when your reports were good, because that always meant you were up to something and working extra hard to cover it up.' He stopped to take a deep, wheezing breath, his eyes narrowing as he remembered. 'Like the term you seduced the headmaster's daughter. When he told me you were going round every night for extra Latin tutorials I knew that something wasn't right.'

Luis smiled blandly. 'It wasn't his daughter, it was his wife. But anyway, you needn't worry this time. I'm behaving impeccably.'

'That's why I'm worried.' King Marcos Fernando picked up a paper from the top of the pile and unfolded it with shaking, frail fingers. Luis felt a tiny pulse of electricity shoot through him as he found himself looking at the picture of him kissing Emily beside the car at the opera house. 'This was your most recent indiscretion, and it was three weeks ago,' his father remarked gruffly, scowling down at the picture. 'Virtually a lifetime by your standards. Oscar Balfour's youngest, isn't she?'

'Emily. That's right.' With heroic effort Luis tore his gaze away from her upturned face in the picture, but it remained imprinted on his mind anyway. 'She's here teaching Luciana ballet.'

'Good.' His father eyed him suspiciously. 'Well, take her out again. You look like you enjoyed it and the press loved it. You have to be careful all this charity work and hospital visiting doesn't make you look too dull. The public won't like that either.'

Luis got abruptly to his feet, thrusting his hands into his

pockets as he strode over to the window and stared unseeingly out over the dispiritingly perfect garden. 'Don't you ever stop thinking of things in terms of how they *look*?' he said with quiet resignation. 'Or what people think?'

'No. That's our life. In our position that's what counts.' From the bed behind him his father's tone was brisk, containing an echo of its old autocracy. Then he added, more thoughtfully, 'This Emily... You're not in love with her, are you?'

'No, of course not.'

The response was instantaneous. Automatic. Meeting his own reflected eyes in the window Luis felt a hollow pang of self-disgust.

'Thank God for that.' King Marcos's voice was breathless with relief, as if Luis had just denied being a serial killer. 'Love is not for us, Luis. You have to marry, of course, and you have to produce an heir, but you look on that as a business deal. A merger, if you like. Love will only make you miserable.'

'How romantic.'

'Romance?' The king made a contemptuous noise. 'Leave romance to Hollywood and fairy tales. The reality of being royal is accepting that you lead a double life. There is business. And there is pleasure. You work hard and you make sacrifices for the business, but you enjoy as much discreet pleasure as you can on the side. If you stick to the rules no one gets hurt.'

The sunny room suddenly felt unbearably hot. Luis could feel a pulse beating in his temples as he slowly turned round to face his father in the bed.

'It's not always that simple though, is it,' he said quietly, leaning back against the windowsill. 'You might want it to be, but it isn't. My mother got hurt.'

As he said it he felt both surprised and oddly relieved. This was forbidden territory, but suddenly Luis knew he had to explore it. He had spent the past fourteen years trying not to think about what had happened, but as Emily had made him see, it had influenced his life and led him down paths he might not have taken if Cassia Cordoba hadn't fallen asleep in the bath and never woken up.

Against the pillows his father's ashen face was hard. 'Yes, but not by me. She got hurt because she broke the rules.'

'How?'

The small silence that followed was filled by the rasping wheeze of the king's breathing. And then he said, 'By falling in love.'

The pulse had increased to a drumbeat. Luis pressed his fingertips absently and fruitlessly against the side of his head, trying to quieten it. 'With someone else?'

'Yes.' King Marcos sighed and looked at Luis with eyes full of regret. 'She wasn't really cut out for royal life—she was too emotional and sensitive—but she was beautiful and came from a good family, so…' He let the sentence trail off with a shrug of his frail shoulders. 'Anyway, things were fine for a while, but then she fell in love with a racing driver.' Luis flinched. 'Their affair went on for years, until he was killed in a race and…'

'She killed herself.' To his own ears his voice sounded hoarse and strange.

'Effectively, yes.' King Marcos's sigh seemed to shake his once-magnificent body to its core, again placing the oxygen tube in jeopardy. 'As you know the official story was that she banged her head in the bath. An accident.'

Luis had known that, but he had also understood without ever being told that his mother's death was somehow inextricably linked to the small brown bottles of pills she carried with her at all times, sliding them from her bag and slipping them swiftly between her lips so often that it never seemed strange. That was how he remembered his mother—vague, distracted, unhappy. Absent even when she was there. The emotional, sensitive girl described by his father sounded like someone else altogether.

Like Emily.

* * *

'No, no, no! Is too *late*!'

The music came to an abrupt halt, as the exasperated voice of the director echoed across the stage. Emily bent her head, her hands on her hips, breathing hard. It was the third time she had mistimed the leap, and she could hardly blame her partner or the director for beginning to lose patience.

'Sorry,' she said, looking at Adriano, who tossed his head and scowled. Tall, Byronically brooding and romantic, the Brazilian National Ballet's principal male was the perfect stereotype of an arrogant *danseur*.

'You maybe have—' he broke off, scowling as he tried to find the right phrase '—overdo it?'

'Yes, I probably have been overdoing it a bit.' Emily bent down, ostentatiously massaging the tops of her legs to hide a sudden secret smile. Not in rehearsals though. Last night had been particularly exhausting, even by Luis's standards, and the ache in her thighs had nothing to do with *grands jetés* and everything to do with *grande passion*. 'Anyway, let's do it again,' she called to the director.

Adriano gave an imperious nod, and said something in incomprehensible Portuguese to Thiago, the diminutive director striding theatrically back towards them as the music started again.

Santosa's *Grande Teatro* was a building of crumbling grandeur and inadequate air conditioning. Emily could feel the sweat running down her spine as she took her opening position for the pas de deux and stared out into the darkness of the auditorium beyond the hot lights. She felt edgy with nerves and the pressure of not screwing up again, and rising up onto her toes she felt the muscles in her inner thighs protest.

Suddenly the memory of wrapping her legs around Luis's waist as he held her and entered her, standing up, came back to her. Oh, God, she thought weakly, trying to force her mind back to the present as her body was shot through with flame, how ironic that Luis had put the passion back into her interpretation, but perfection and precision seemed to have gone out of the window.

Discipline, focus, control. Arms, feet, spine. Ruthlessly she centred her attention, balancing herself for the leap. This time the timing was exact, and Adriano caught her, his hands spanning her midriff as he lowered her gently back onto her pointes.

They held the pose as the pas de deux came to an end, their chests rising and falling in unison. Pressed against the muscular arc of Adriano's body, Emily felt light headed for a moment as she recalled the way she and Luis had eventually fallen onto the bed, breathless and exhilarated, her flushed cheek pressed against his damp skin, her whole body spreadeagled over him.

The music finished. *'Perfeito!'* cried Thiago, springing forward with an expansive sweep of his arms, while from the auditorium behind him came the sound of clapping.

He whirled round in surprise and affront at having his rehearsal interrupted. Emily squinted out into the gloom and saw someone get up from a seat about halfway back and step into the aisle. Someone tall, and broad shouldered, with the arrogant, loping, predatory walk of a tiger.

Or a wolf.

Thiago's outraged squawk ceased abruptly, and became apologetic and ingratiating as Prince Luis came forward into the lights. Adriano sprang away from her as if she were red hot, backing off and simultaneously bending into a deep bow. 'Your Highness…'

Luis nodded curtly, his face oddly expressionless.

'Forgive me for intruding on your rehearsal.' His voice, even when speaking such bland courtesies, made the hairs rise on the back of her neck. 'It's coming together.' His gaze flickered briefly in her direction and heat bloomed beneath her skin. 'Sehora Balfour is doing well.'

'Sim,' Thiago agreed with a sigh, 'plenty of—how you say it?—*paixão.*'

'Passion,' Luis translated neutrally. In the footlights his eyes gleamed gold, and a muscle twitched above his jaw.

Thiago planted his hands on his hips and looked at Emily appraisingly. 'But only a week to performance, so we must take that passion and add to it *precisão*.'

'Not today.' Luis shot Adriano a cool glance. 'I have to take Senhora Balfour away, I'm afraid. Important business.'

'So what's the problem? Is it Luciana?'

Across the table Emily's blue eyes were clouded with anxiety, but Luis took a sip of coffee before answering. They were sitting in a tiny dark bar, in a little side street off Santosa's main square. It wasn't exactly the Ritz, but Luis had known the owner for many years and trusted him to keep the paparazzi out. At a table by the door his two bodyguards drank coffee and failed to look inconspicuous.

'No, Luciana's fine.' He put the cup back on the saucer with a clatter and ran his hand over his unshaven jaw. He felt tense and edgy with unfamiliar emotions that he was sickeningly aware of but couldn't bear to examine. The feeling reminded him of when he'd come off a motorbike a few years ago—those few moments of watching the blood seeping through his shirt, feeling the pain but not wanting to look at the wound. 'I just came from visiting my father.'

'Is he…getting worse?'

'No. On the contrary, he was better than I'd seen him for a while. Certainly more talkative.'

Her eyes were full of compassion. 'That's good, isn't it?'

'Maybe,' he said tersely, picking up a sugar cube and crumbling it between his fingers. 'But weird. As I told you, in our family we don't go in for talking much.' It was good that he knew, good that he finally understood the shadow that had hung over his childhood, but it had unsettled him more than he cared to admit. That's why he'd gone to find Emily. He wanted the reassurance of her normality and straightforwardness. Brushing the sugar from his fingers he leaned restlessly back in his seat. 'So, how was the rehearsal?'

She shrugged, a shadow passing over her open face. 'As you saw. I have the passion nailed and now I need to work on precision.'

'You certainly do have the passion nailed,' Luis drawled acidly. 'What do you and *Adriano* do for an encore? Have sex in the middle of the stage?'

He had a sudden dizzying flashback to that night in England, when he'd so arrogantly, so bloody calculatingly begun to seduce her in the hotel. *Jealousy is a nasty disease to which, thankfully, I'm completely immune.* His cold, complacent words came back to him and he recognized the devastating justice of the situation he now found himself in. Turned inside out by jealousy for a *dancer*, for pity's sake.

'I have enough sex at the moment, thank you,' she said softly, and for a moment her eyes met his across the table and he was gripped by a strong urge to pick her up and haul her back to his bed. *I don't*, he wanted to say. It felt like he could never have enough of her.

'Anyway—' a flush of pink had spread across her cheekbones and she dropped her gaze '—I wanted to talk to you about Luciana. It's her birthday next week.'

Luis was relieved at the change of subject. 'Of course,' he said tersely. And almost a year since Rico and Christiana died.

'Well, since she doesn't really have any friends her own age I wondered if we could do something with her, instead of a party. Something fun.' She looked at him under her eyelashes. 'Something *normal*.'

'Do you have something in mind?'

'I do, but you're not going to like it…' With a rueful smile she stooped down, reaching beneath the table and wincing slightly. 'Sorry, my feet are killing me.'

Frowning, Luis glanced down. Under the table he could see that she had slipped her shoes off and was rubbing her toes. A bolt of pure, blinding lust shot through him. 'Go on,' he rasped.

'Well, I thought…' As she uncrossed her legs her bare foot

brushed his knee and he caught hold of it under the table. She smiled, a slow, spreading smile that made the sun rise in her clear blue eyes and heated his blood. 'I thought…' she repeated, her voice throaty with undisguised desire as his fingers gently massaged her instep, 'that we could…'

He raised his eyebrows, enjoying her unraveling. 'Yes…'

She hesitated. 'I don't want you to say no,' she whispered, sliding down in her chair a little, pushing back her loose, silken hair with her fingers, her eyes not leaving his. There was a wicked glitter in them, and suddenly he wasn't holding her foot any more. She had twisted it neatly from his grasp with a flick of her ankle and slid it between his thighs.

He tensed, instantly rock hard as her strong, supple toes flexed against him.

'Promise you won't say no,' she breathed, her eyes laughing, burning into his.

'*Atrevido,*' he murmured hoarsely. Light-headed with want he glanced across at the oblivious bodyguards who were sprawled at their table, chatting desultorily. He looked back at Emily. Her perfect heart-shaped face was composed and serene. Only her eyes, which had darkened to the colour of sapphires and were sparkling feverishly, gave her away. 'I can't imagine,' he said in a voice like honey and gravel, 'saying no to anything you could suggest right now. So tell me.'

She smiled, wickedly and delightfully, and he swallowed back a groan as he felt her other foot slip between his thighs. 'Camping. I want to take her camping. In a tent. On the beach.'

CHAPTER THIRTEEN

'OK, NOW both of you, close your eyes.'

Emily and Luciana looked at each other, excitement shimmering between them on the soft late-afternoon heat. 'Go on.' Emily grinned. 'You first, and then I will.'

Luciana screwed her eyes up very tightly as if she was afraid they might accidentally spring open. Emily glanced up at Luis.

'You too, Miss Balfour,' he said sternly, taking her face between his hands and brushing his thumbs down over her eyelids. 'And keep them shut until I say so.'

The sand was soft beneath her feet as Luis took each of their hands and pulled them up the last steep bit of the dune. The incline levelled off as they reached the summit and Emily felt the breeze lift her hair and the sun warm her face, and she heard the sigh of the waves and breathed in the evocative salt and ozone scents of the sea.

'Now,' he said quietly. 'Open.'

It was the Arabian Nights, or Camelot, laid out below them on the beach. A number of round white canvas tents were clustered together on the sand, pink pennants flying from their turrets, bunting and balloons strung between them. Luciana was standing transfixed, her hands pressed to her mouth, her eyes brilliant with tears of astonishment and delight.

Emily knew exactly how she felt.

'Is it real?' Luciana whispered. 'Am I really sleeping there tonight?'

'You bet,' Luis said, and Emily's throat constricted as she heard the note of gravelly emotion in his voice. 'Because you're the birthday girl. Go and look at your bedroom—you might find some people you know down there.'

And she was off, running down the slope of the dune in the little red shorts and striped T-shirt Emily had bought her as part of her birthday present, her hair flying out behind her. Only then did Emily turn to Luis, laughing as the sentimental tears that shimmered in her eyes spilled over. 'It's incredible. Absolutely perfect. *Thank you*.'

'I'm glad it meets with your approval,' he said drily.

'Oh, it does. Very much.'

She rose up on her tiptoes to press a kiss to his mouth, but instantly he stepped away. A tiny beat of disappointment went through her. 'Careful.' He gestured down the beach with a nod of his head. 'We have an audience.'

From out of the tents Tomás had emerged, looking almost unrecognisable out of his ubiquitous suit and tie. With him was a pretty, plump blonde woman who she assumed was Valentina holding a chubby baby on one hip, and Elena and Paloma, two of the junior nannies from the palace. Senhora Costa, mercifully, did not seem to be in evidence, but there were several young men in shorts and T-shirts whom Emily couldn't place.

'Inviting half of the security force was the only way I could get Tomás and the chief of security to agree to this,' Luis said, following her gaze, and she realised that the tanned, relaxed boys down there were the bodyguards she was used to seeing in headsets and uniforms, opening doors for her and following Luis like shadows. Now, here in the fading afternoon sun as they went forward to greet Luciana they looked human for the first time.

'Was it very difficult?' she asked guiltily.

'Put it this way, it'll make any future diplomatic dealings I may have with fascist dictators and volatile despots look like schoolboy stuff.' He gave her a crooked smile. 'Come on. Let me show you to your boudoir, your ladyship. And let's get this party started.'

They played rounders and had piggyback races, with the pretty young nannies shrieking excitedly on the backs of the younger bodyguards. Emily stood on the finish line taking photographs as Luis charged across it with Luciana clinging to him like a little monkey, her face alight with happiness.

He had long since discarded his T-shirt and, wearing only faded surf shorts, his tawny hair glinting gold in the sun it was hard to imagine the responsibility that rested on his beautiful, butterscotch-brown shoulders. And yet, Emily thought with a wrench of visceral yearning, it was also impossible to forget that he was what he was. Royal. Special. Separate. It was in every powerful inch of him, every self-assured move and graceful gesture.

She thought back to the night in the restaurant, when they'd played that silly game about animals—the bitterness in his voice when he'd said he wasn't regal enough to be a lion—but looking at him now in the low, syrupy sunlight, that was exactly what he reminded her of. The wolf had emerged from the shadows, and he was stronger, prouder and even more compelling.

After the games Tomás lit a fire and Valentina cooked sausages and steaks while Luciana played with baby Gracia. One of the tents had been set up as a bar and kitchen, and Matheus, Luciana's favourite bodyguard, made her a cola float which he embellished with a tiny pink paper umbrella and presented to her with a flourish. He'd also brought an iPod, and as the sun changed from primrose yellow to deep blush pink music filled the warm evening and Luis opened champagne.

Instinctively Emily had kept a distance from him, but suddenly he was standing in front of her, holding out a slim glass. Their eyes locked as she took it from him, her stomach disappearing with longing as their fingers touched.

'Thank you.'

'Thank *you*,' he said ironically. 'This is all your idea.'

'But this is more than I ever could have dreamed up…' She waved her glass in an arc that took in the tents, the deserted beach, the rose-petal sun sliding down towards the glittering sea. 'You've taken my idea and made it magical. Luciana's having the time of her life.'

His face was very still, and very, very beautiful, as he looked out across the ocean. 'I hope so,' he said, and his voice was low and raw.

Behind them someone turned up the music and Luciana was calling her name. Reluctantly tearing her gaze from his she turned round.

'Emily, listen!' Luciana squealed, 'Matheus has the music for our dance! Let's do it! Let's do it now!'

Sure enough the *Waltz of the Flowers* from *The Nutcracker*, with its associations of home and Christmas, was floating incongruously over the tropical white sand. Smiling, Emily took a mouthful of champagne and then handed her glass back to Luis before knotting her faded checked shirt over her midriff and going to join Luciana.

Luciana's face was set in a frown of concentration as she went through her carefully rehearsed routine, and Emily danced around her, the silken sand flying from her bare feet with each fouetté. At the end everyone clapped madly, and Luciana glowed with pride.

'Now you,' she begged Emily. 'Do yours!'

'No, no.' Laughing, Emily dropped a kiss on her head and went back over to Luis to reclaim her champagne. 'This is a party— we should all dance. Matheus, do you have any party music?'

'Of course!' A moment later the low pulsing beat of the samba filled the warm evening, and Matheus went back to Luciana and took both her hands. 'I show Your Highness,' he joked. 'And then you can teach Senhora Balfour how we dance in Santosa.'

'Uh-uh,' said Luis, very close to her ear. 'That's definitely going to be my privilege.'

Elena and Paloma had been claimed by their bodyguards, and Tomás was drawing a laughing, protesting Valentina forwards. The music was insistent, infectious, and Emily couldn't have resisted its persuasive beat, even if it hadn't been for Luis's hands on her waist.

He was, she discovered with a debilitating kick of desire, a brilliant dancer. Pushing his fingers into the back pockets of her tight denim shorts he pulled her hips close to his so that they were swaying and undulating in unison, their upper bodies almost motionless, their gazes locked smokily together. For a long time they danced like that as the sun flamed lower, a blood orange dripping into the sea, turning his bare chest to beaten bronze, his eyes to liquid gold.

'You're a natural samba dancer,' Luis murmured, his voice warm and husky with approval.

'Perhaps I've found my niche.' She smiled straight into his eyes. 'I'm rubbish at ballet these days. No precision. No control.'

'I *love* your lack of control.'

Instantly her smile faded and her body turned fluid with desire. 'Luis, I—'

'Shhh.' His eyes were hooded as he placed a finger on her lips. 'Not here. Not now.' Around them the party continued, and he let her go and took a step back. 'I think I should go and dance with the birthday girl for a little while, don't you?'

Emily nodded mutely, half relieved at the respite from the exhausting onslaught of desire, half desolate at his abrupt withdrawal. She should be used to it by now, she told herself despairingly, watching him go over to Luciana. She should be used to wanting him—*all* of him—and having him always elude her.

Because that was the great flaw in the centre of her joy. He had awoken her, introduced her to pleasure and excitement she had never even previously imagined, and she had opened herself up to him completely, heart and mind and body and soul. While he…he remained as distant and unknowable as the moon.

Luciana's delighted laughter rose into the soft apricot

evening as Luis picked her up and twirled her round, her hands small on his muscular shoulders. Emily swallowed the lump in her throat, trying to summon a smile, like everyone else. Even though she'd just realised she was in love with the Crown Prince of Santosa and there wasn't a chance that he loved her back.

Meaningless sex, that's all it was for him.

Gorgeous, mind-blowing, life altering. But not enough.

Later, after Luciana's birthday candles and the orange glow of the sun had both been extinguished and the dancing had given way to stories around the campfire, a yawning Luciana was put to bed in her silken-draped tent. Ducking through the doorway, Luis went in to say goodnight to her. She was almost asleep, and as he bent down beside the little camp bed he was hit by a rush of emotion so powerful it made it hard to breathe for a second.

Guilt. Always guilt, but now so much more.

'Thank you for a lovely party,' she whispered, the soft glow of the lantern beside her reflected in her shining eyes.

He smiled. 'It's my pleasure. Did you have a nice birthday?'

'The best,' she said fiercely. 'The best birthday *ever.*'

Her answer, and the emphasis with which she spoke, took him by surprise. 'Good,' he said quietly, straightening up. 'I'm glad.'

For a moment he hovered, the pressure of things he wanted to say but didn't know how swelling in his throat, and then there was a rustle of canvas as Emily came in. She looked at him. In the cool, clear pools of her eyes he felt all his troubles could be washed away, and as she came towards the bed she brushed his arm with her fingertips and his throat closed and words deserted him anyway.

With a last smile at Luciana he went out. Everyone was sitting around the campfire a little distance away from the tents, but Luis didn't go over. Picking up a bottle of beer he headed instead in the other direction, towards the cliffs at the far end of the cove. Ever since they arrived he had been aware of their dark bulk and had tried to ignore it, but he knew now that he could put it off no longer. He had to go down there, today of all days. Luciana's birthday.

Her best birthday ever, he thought with a fresh burst of surprise. He was ashamed to remember how in previous years the date hadn't really meant much to him, but he'd assumed that Rico and Christiana would have done something to make it special. But then maybe he didn't know his brother as well as he'd thought. He'd always been in awe of Rico for his absolute dedication to duty, but maybe that had been incompatible with being a hands-on, loving father.

Without thinking he had headed down to the water's edge, walking along the hard sand with the lacy edges of the waves flapping gently over the tops of his feet. Ahead of him the cliffs rose up, huge and black and menacing. As he got closer to them the air got distinctly cooler, as if Rico's restless spirit was lurking there.

Taking a mouthful of beer he turned away from the sea and headed up the beach, his feet sinking into the powdery sand as his eyes scanned the gloom for the huge mound of rock that he had privately marked out as Rico's monument. Locating it he made his way towards it and lowered himself down onto the sand at its foot.

It was surprisingly warm against his bare back. He took another swig of beer from the bottle and looked back along the darkening beach. The glow of the campfire seemed a long, long way away, the figures around it just indistinguishable shapes, but inevitably he found himself automatically searching for Emily amongst them.

Emily. Just saying her name inside his head made his pulse quicken and his body harden. *Deus*, it was like being under some kind of spell. She had got inside him, and if he had found it hard to resist her before, now he had touched and tasted and possessed her it was almost impossible.

What had started as a relationship he had been ordered to fake for the sake of his public image had become something that was fundamental to the most private, personal part of himself. That was why he wanted to keep it secret, in some kind of attempt to protect it. And her. Because the moment anyone suspected that it was genuine, it would be over. As vividly as if she had been there, whispering it to him in the gathering gloom, he recalled Josefina's comment about his private life *It's now a political matter rather than simply a personal one.*

A movement a little distance away caught his eye. Someone was walking along the sand through the veils of milky twilight towards him, and he turned away facing out to sea, resentment and bitterness sweeping through him. It would be Tomás or one of the bodyguards, come to find him in their constant quest to protect him from bands of drug-crazed terrorists, rabid republicans, mentally unstable fanatics. What they couldn't seem to grasp was that he wasn't remotely bothered about any of those, but what terrified him was the very real danger of being locked into a lifetime of lies and emptiness.

'Luis?'

Emily's voice—soft, tentative and so sexy it hurt. He turned his head. She was standing a few yards away, her long bare legs in the tiny denim shorts silhouetted against the glow of the fire in the distance, her face indistinguishable in the shadows.

'Yes, I'm here.' His voice sounded rusty and cracked.

'Do you want to be alone? I wondered where you were, but if you'd rather be—'

'No.' That's exactly what he'd come down here for, what he thought he wanted, but now he knew he'd much rather be with her. Hell, what was happening to him lately? He didn't even know himself any more.

'Actually,' he said sardonically, 'I came down here to be with Rico. This is the place where his helicopter came down, almost exactly a year ago, so I thought I ought to come and have a drink with him.'

He raised his half-empty bottle. A second later another one

clinked against it in the half-light and he realised that she was carrying one too. 'Can I join you both?' she asked quietly.

'I'd like that.'

She sat down on the sand beside him, not close enough to be touching, but just her presence seemed to enfold him in an odd sense of calm. For a moment neither of them spoke, and the only sound was the rhythmic breaking of the waves, and beneath that the gentler sigh of their breathing. In and out. Together.

'Tell me about him,' she murmured after a while. 'Tell me what Rico was like.'

'What was he like?' Luis echoed, his grip tightening around the bottle in his hand. 'Nothing like me, is the short answer. He was…always *the same*.' He spoke slowly and with difficulty, realizing that it was an odd way to describe his brother yet suddenly understanding that this was significant. 'All the time, whoever he was with. There was no difference between the man he was in private and the persona he presented to the world. Everything about who he was came naturally to him.'

'Who he was? You mean the heir?'

'Yes, just like everything about being the spare came naturally to me…' Acrid self-loathing rose up inside him, dripping from every word and almost choking him. 'Taking the privilege without taking any responsibility, enjoying the deference of my title without doing anything to earn it. But Rico was the opposite.'

'But you're taking that responsibility now.' It was a statement, not a question, and she made it with a serene certainty that was infinitely soothing. Until he remembered what he'd done and the doors of his private prison slammed shut again.

'On the surface, yes. But everything in me rebels against it. I'll never be able to do it wholeheartedly.'

Not like she would. *Whatever she does she does passionately, with her whole heart and soul.* It seemed like a lifetime ago that he'd had that conversation with Oscar, and yet every word was still etched indelibly onto his memory. Whether he wanted it there or not.

His stomach clenched with helpless desire as he watched her raise the beer bottle to her lips, close them around it and take a mouthful. 'Do you have to do it at all, then?' she asked softly. 'Can't you—'

'Walk away?' His short laugh rang with icy despair. 'Not an option. I just have to accept the stage management and the manipulation of the truth and the blatant bloody lies the palace press office spin in the name of my "image".'

'But why?' She had moved while he was talking, rising up so she was half kneeling beside his outstretched legs, facing him. She still had her shirt knotted beneath her breasts from when they'd danced earlier. 'Why can't you just be yourself?'

'Because the real me isn't up to the job, I'm afraid.' With difficulty he wrenched his gaze away from her flat, smooth midriff and gave a twisted smile. 'Being royal is essentially like being a character in a fairy tale—you only exist as long as people believe in you. So you have to make sure they believe, and in the age of mobile-phone cameras and the Internet that's pretty impossible because there are people lurking round every corner waiting to show how human you are.' He took a mouthful of beer, and added with a weary attempt at humour, 'Let's face it, even you had given up believing in fairy tales.'

'Ah, but I believe again now,' she said softly. 'Thanks to you—the *real* you.' Without getting up she shifted her position so that in one neat movement she was on her knees straddling his outstretched legs. 'You're wrong, you know, about not being up to it. You might not be the same kind of king as your father was and your brother would have been, but if you do it your way you'll be brilliant. You'll make everyone believe, like me.'

Luis stiffened, trying to suppress the lust that surged though him. He turned his head, away from her searchlight gaze, and gave a rueful, mocking laugh. 'I can't sleep with everyone.'

Her smile widened and she trailed a languid finger down his chest. 'That's not what you would have said when I first met you...'

'No,' he said tersely. 'But everything's changed since then. I'm not like that any more.'

'Because you're taking on the responsibility of—'

'*No.*' The word sounded like a curse in the velvet twilight. Heart hammering, adrenaline stinging through him, Luis pulled his legs from beneath her and got to his feet. 'Because it was *my fault*,' he ground out through gritted teeth, raking his fingers through his hair. 'What happened was my fault, and that's something I have to live with every day for the rest of my hollow sham of a double life.'

She had got up and was beside him, reaching out to him. 'What do you mean?'

He shrugged her off. 'I was supposed to go to the award ceremony that Rico and Christiana attended that night. It was in *my* schedule. *My* engagement. But so was judging the Miss Santosa contest earlier that day.' Disgust rang through every word and he turned to face her, needing to see the reaction on her face. 'The winner was exceptionally pretty and exceptionally grateful. I rang Rico from the Jacuzzi of the honeymoon suite and asked him to do the award ceremony in my place.'

'*Oh, Luis…*'

It was a whisper on the still air, barely audible above the sigh of the sea.

'No, please. Don't say anything. There's nothing *to* say, really. So, now you know. I killed my brother and his wife, and in doing so I not only destroyed their lives and Luciana's life, but I pretty comprehensively screwed up my own too, which is only fair.'

'You didn't kill them.'

She had come to stand behind him now, and a violent tremor went through him as she laid her palms flat on his back, on his shoulder blades. 'Not with my own hands,' he said savagely. 'But it amounts to the same thing.' He broke off and gave a bitter laugh. 'At least I'm sure that's how Luciana will see it when she's old enough to understand. That's why I didn't want to get close to her. Because then, when she finds out what I did to her parents, it'll feel like even more of a betrayal.'

'You haven't betrayed her.' Emily's voice was low and firm, and as she spoke her hands moved across his shoulders so she was gripping him, hard. 'And you've given her more warmth and affection in the past few weeks than she's had in five years before that.' Her grip tightened. 'She *loves* you.'

'No.' The word was wrenched out of him. With a jerk of his shoulders he twisted free of her grasp and turned to face her, shaking his head. 'Don't say that. I don't deserve it.'

Slowly, emphatically, she nodded, her eyes burning into his through the violet night. 'Yes, you *do*. What happened was one of those random, appalling acts that none of us can control. The only thing we have any power over is how we respond, and you responded by becoming stronger, braver, more honourable. That's how you won her love.' She paused for a heartbeat. 'And mine too.'

'Emily, *no*…' It was the ferocious growl of an animal in pain, but she didn't flinch. She simply raised her hands in silent surrender.

'Sorry. I know I'm breaking all the rules by saying it, but I'm no good at pretending or manipulating the truth. I love you.'

Before he could stop himself he had taken her by the shoulders. *'Don't,'* he rasped, shaking her so she stumbled against him. 'Because if you do your life will be destroyed too, and I can't…I don't think I could stand that…'

But it was a mistake to have touched her. At the feel of her body against his bare skin reason deserted him and suddenly he wasn't holding her away from him any more. His arms were around her, clutching him with the feverish desperation of a drowning man reaching for a raft. Her hands were cradling his face, her mouth hot against his, her miraculous body pressing against him until they were almost one. Almost…

He hauled himself away, leaving Emily gasping, reeling, frantic. 'Luis—'

'No.' He staggered backwards, pressing his clenched fists

against his temples. '*Christo*, I was wrong to do this to you. Nothing can come of it, you know that, don't you? There's *no future* in this.'

Emily's heart was beating so hard it racked her whole body with every painful thud. 'Of course,' she said in a voice that shook with need. 'Meaningless sex. We said it all along. And right now I don't care about the future, I just care about now. Tonight, and however long this lasts.'

For a long moment he didn't move. Bare chested and beautiful, in the dying light he looked like a tortured saint. Emily felt like Faust, signing his terrible deal with the devil, a short spell of earthly bliss at the expense of an eternity of torment.

But as Luis took her hand and led her silently up the dark beach she couldn't be sorry. And as he laid her down amongst the layers of rugs and blankets in his tent and undressed her, holding her, stroking her with his hands, worshipping her with his mouth and his tongue, she felt like she was dancing with the angels.

Her dreams were hazy, suffused with rapture and the constant sigh of the sea. She awoke at first light, and before she opened her eyes she was aware of Luis's body, warm and hard against her back, his arms tight around her, and she smiled.

Outside she could hear voices, low and grave, and realised that must have been what woke her. And then the tent flap was parting to reveal a slice of colourless sky, and Tomás's face. It too was drained of colour.

Behind her Luis sat up, letting her go.

'I'm sorry to disturb you, Your Highness. I'm afraid it's your father.'

CHAPTER FOURTEEN

THE machine that was keeping King Marcos Fernando alive was slowly and relentlessly driving Luis mad. It emitted a beeping sound at a pitch that seemed to be exactly calibrated to cause the most discomfort to the human ear as it measured each laboured breath.

The room was impossibly hot. Getting stiffly up from the plastic chair Luis felt the sweat cool in the small of his back as he went over to the window, parting the slats of the blind to look out. The sun was high in a hazy sky. How many hours had he been there now? he wondered bleakly. How many thousand times had he heard that bloody beep, and how long was it since he had woken up with his cheek against Emily's hair and her body clasped against his?

He rested his head against the glass and closed eyes that felt gritty with exhaustion and wondered if he was going out of his mind.

'Your Highness?'

Tomás stood in the doorway, glancing anxiously over to the still figure in the bed before turning back to Luis. 'Perhaps it's time for a break, sir—some coffee or something. I brought you a change of clothes.'

Luis looked down, realizing with a beat of surprise that he was still wearing yesterday's surf shorts and T-shirt. 'Does it really matter what I'm wearing?' he asked wearily, looking at the suit carrier draped over Tomás's arm. 'At least this is cool.' And a whisper of Emily's perfume still clung to it.

'The press, sir. Obviously they're outside, and that… Well, it doesn't quite give the right impression at a time like this.'

The right impression. Of course. Luis's chest constricted with impotent fury as he followed Tomás out into the lobby of their private suite and into a small sitting room on the other side.

Tomás laid the suit carrier down on the sofa and set about filling the kettle on the countertop. Encased once more in tailored grey flannel it was impossible to connect him with the man who had danced on the beach with his barefoot wife a little over twelve hours ago.

'I've just come from a meeting with Josefina and the King's private secretary,' he said. 'We felt we had no alternative but to cancel tomorrow's jubilee celebration.'

Luis nodded numbly, peeling the T-shirt off over his head. A light scattering of sand fell onto the carpet. The only thought that formed in his head with any clarity was the fact that he wouldn't have to watch Emily dancing in the arms of another man.

'I also spoke to the Duchess de Mesa, sir. She's flying out as soon as possible.'

'Why?'

Tomás turned and held out a mug of steaming black coffee. Luis didn't take it.

Very carefully Tomás put it on the low table beside the sofa. 'Josefina feels that in the difficult days ahead, it would be good to have her here. In the background, as your f—'

He faltered, unable to meet Luis's eye.

'My future *wife*.' Luis almost spat the words. Prison doors seemed to be slamming behind him, shutting out the light, making it difficult to breathe. Suddenly choking on despair he leaned against the wall, bracing his arms against it as if he could push it back, give himself more air. In that moment he wanted Emily so much that he thought he might black out.

'So that's it, is it?' he said, in a voice of infinite desolation.

'It's one relentless march now from my father's funeral to my wedding.' His business-merger marriage. And from there to his own funeral, whenever that might be. All of a sudden it hardly seemed to matter. The only thing that was certain was that there would be precious little happiness along the way.

'It's been planned that way for a long time, sir,' Tomás said quietly. 'You know that. It comes with the role.'

He flinched as Luis smashed his fist against the wall. 'And what if I don't want *the role*?'

Tomás blanched. 'Then you would have to abdicate, sir. And Princess Luciana would take the throne.'

Utterly defeated, Luis slumped against the wall. He had a sudden image of Luciana's dark curls bouncing, her little arms windmilling with joy as she ran down the sand dune yesterday. Something normal and fun, that's what Emily had wanted to give her and she had adored every second. How much opportunity would she get to be normal if she was queen? How many chances to have fun?

From the direction of the King's room across the lobby the electronic beep that had provided the steady background to their conversation suddenly intensified to a persistent whine. There was a flurry of activity and a surge of running feet outside, and without thinking Luis found himself rushing across the lobby towards his father's room. The bed was surrounded by white-coated figures silently checking machinery and adjusting tubes, their faces as blank and grave as angels.

And as he leaned against the door frame watching them, he was suddenly reminded of the morning when his mother's body was discovered—standing in the doorway of her bedroom and looking into the bathroom beyond as the paramedics lifted her from the water, checking for a pulse, trying to restart her heart. *She wasn't really cut out for royal life,* his father had said. *She was too emotional and sensitive.* She had been dragged into a life of duty and it had killed her.

He couldn't do that to Emily.

He turned and walked away, his jaw set like steel against the wave of total desolation that smashed through him. There was no escape.

Behind him the electronic noise that had filled his head and sliced through his thoughts for such a long time abruptly ceased, so that there was suddenly nothing. An absence of any sound, any feeling, any hope.

And then Tomás was beside him, pale and composed.

'He's gone.' He bowed his head gravely. 'I'm so sorry, Your Majesty.'

'Would you like some tea and biscuits, Senhora Balfour?'

Emily blinked, dragging her gaze back from the bright square of sky beyond the window to the immaculately made-up face of the woman who stood behind the desk in the palace's press office.

'Oh. Yes,' she stuttered dazedly. 'Yes, thank you, that would be…good.'

The realization that she was hungry broke upon her with a flash of surprise. Since they left the beach at first light the day had taken on an odd, end-of-the-world feeling of silence and waiting, in which ordinary things like food and drink had had no place. Here, in the bright, efficient room, the feeling receded a little.

'Thank you for coming, Senhora.' The woman—Josefina something, she had introduced herself as—was smiling at Emily now, with glossy mulberry-coloured lips. Emily wasn't sure how to reply. She hadn't been aware of having a choice about obeying the summons to the press office.

'No problem,' she muttered, suddenly distinctly aware that she was still wearing yesterday's frayed denim shorts and checked shirt. 'Why did you want to see me?'

Josefina sat down, looking at Emily with an expression of intense pity. 'I'm afraid I have to tell you that the King died a short time ago.'

Emily heard the words, but it took a moment for their

weighty implications to sink in. As they did she found herself stumbling to her feet, her mouth opening and her head spinning. She had to find something acceptable to say to the woman opposite, something correct and respectful, but all she could think of was…

'Luis. I need to see him.'

The words came out in a dry croak, and instantly she knew she had made a mistake. Josefina's face hardened.

'I'm afraid that's out of the question,' she snapped, and then visibly reined back her impatience. 'Please, sit down. Prince Luis is king now, and this is going to be a very difficult time for him. It needs to be handled very…sensitively and carefully.'

Emily sank back onto her chair, gripped by a growing sense of dread. 'I don't understand.'

Josefina sighed, folding her hands together on the desk. 'King Marcos Fernando was enormously popular amongst the people, and his passing will cause genuine grief, especially coming so soon after Prince Rico's death,' she explained, as if she was talking to a small child. 'For the past year, since he became the crown prince, we have been working extensively on Prince Luis's public image, in anticipation of this. Opinion polls show that what we've achieved has been a little short of miraculous. The public now regard him almost as favourably as they did Prince Rico.'

She looked at Emily across the table, as if waiting for a response. Emily would have obliged had she had any clue as to what the correct one would be.

'I'm afraid I don't know what this has to do with me…'

The mulberry lips widened into a patronising smile. 'Well, of course, to a certain extent we have you to thank for it.' Suddenly businesslike Josefina seized the computer mouse and clicked briskly, then swivelled the monitor screen around so Emily could see it. 'Involving you in the PR campaign was a gamble, but one that has proved surprisingly successful.'

'PR campaign?' Emily whispered, through lips that were

suddenly dry. A succession of images flashed up on the screen before her eyes—newspaper front pages, showing various pictures of her with Luis. Kissing by the steps of the plane when she'd arrived in Santosa. Side by side in the back of a car. Shot with a long lens getting into another car. With Luciana. Arriving at the opera house on the night of the ballet. Leaving later, Luis holding her face between his hands as he kissed her.

His words from last night came back to her, along with a clammy wave of nausea. *I just have to accept the stage management and the manipulation of the truth and the blatant bloody lies the palace press office spin in the name of my 'image.'* He'd been trying to tell her, she realised now. Trying to break it to her that everything that had happened between them was part of that stage management.

'We needed someone who would provide a complete contrast with the kind of…*lifestyle* with which the Prince had formerly been associated, and you've been perfect.' Josefina bestowed on Emily the smile of a headmistress handing out gold stars for good work. 'Unfortunately now, things have changed again,' she went on, the smile fading slightly as if she'd decided Emily's performance hadn't actually made the grade after all. 'And now the Prince is to become the King, we need to start thinking long term. About his marriage.'

The door opened and a girl came in with a tray of tea and biscuits. Emily's stomach gave an ominous lurch.

'Obrigado, Ana.' Josefina dismissed the girl and turned her attention back to Emily. 'Now is the time that we need to introduce—in a very low-key way, of course—the woman who will in due course become Queen of Santosa. We'd like her to be in the background, unobtrusively supporting the Prince through this difficult time.'

Everything was going way too fast. Suddenly drenched in sweat Emily clutched the arms of the chair, fighting faintness, unable to take in the fact that the woman in front of her with the black, spiky eyelashes and the painted mouth was talking about Luis. Luis, in whose arms she had woken up only a couple of hours ago, who now it seemed was virtually engaged to someone else.

'Who is she?' she said, in a voice that sounded nothing like her own.

'The Duchess de Mesa comes from an old and very distinguished Portuguese family,' Josefina explained smugly, pouring tea. 'She's been being groomed for this role for many years. She's the ideal person to be at his side both now and in the future.'

Emily wished she hadn't asked. With nerveless fingers she picked at the frayed edge of her shorts, trying to take it all in, but it was like looking at a mosaic with a magnifying glass, and she could only see one meaningless piece at a time. 'What about me?' she whispered. 'What about the jubilee event?'

'Regrettably it's going to have to be cancelled. You're welcome to stay in Santosa if you wish, but it might be slightly…*awkward* if you were to continue to remain at the palace after the Duchess arrives.'

Emily nodded. She felt a split second of ridiculous relief that she wouldn't have to dance the pas de deux before horror descended on her, blanking out everything else. *It's over*, she thought in disbelief. *It's over already*. The period of grace she had bargained for had come to an end before she had even had a chance to catch her breath, and now the devil had come to take his payment.

'I'm sorry, *Senhora*. It was not supposed to happen like this.' Josefina spoke carefully, her words faintly tinged with guilt. 'The prince was so sure we could keep all this…under control. Hurting you was the last thing we wanted.'

'I understand,' Emily whispered.

And she did. Luis had all but told her all this himself. *I was wrong to do this to you,* he'd said last night, his voice raw with remorse. He had never deceived her. She had known the risks and she had plunged in anyway. Into the wild woods.

Emily got to her feet, but as she did so she caught the scent of Luis on her skin and her legs almost gave way again beneath her. The door suddenly seemed a long way away and it was all she could do to get herself across the room and open it.

'I am grateful to you for making it easier for him,' Josefina said, as she reached it. 'I had thought you might be difficult about going, but I can see I underestimated you. Thank you.' For the first time she sounded completely sincere. Sincere and relieved. But when Emily looked back she had already moved on and was scribbling something on a piece of paper while reaching for the phone.

Out in the corridor with its rows of windows pouring sunlight onto the polished parquet Emily took a deep, tearing breath and had to lean against the wall to steady herself. Someone was walking towards her and she ducked her head. Her life might be over but she still had enough pride to feel self-conscious about falling apart in front of palace staff.

But through the blur of tears there was something about the approaching figure that made her heart stop. And then he spoke, and his voice was clipped, English and wrenchingly familiar.

'Emily? My God…darling.'

She gave a whimper, her last shreds of self-control snapping as she ran forward into Oscar Balfour's outstretched arms.

'Oh, sweetheart,' he murmured, his voice cracking with emotion.

'Daddy,' she sobbed, breathing in the familiar scent of cologne and Jermyn Street shaving soap. 'You're here—oh, thank God, you're here. Please, Daddy—can I come home?'

CHAPTER FIFTEEN

AND in the end this was all there was, Luis thought numbly.

A narrow bed. A sheet folded neatly. A sense of things finished.

Or that's how it was for his father. A life well lived. A job well done. A grieving public and an official period of mourning. A son who couldn't feel much at all.

He dropped his head into his hands, and anyone passing the door would have thought that he was stricken with loss for his father, when the truth was he had barely known him. Marcos Fernando had been a King before he was a parent. He had been someone whose picture appeared on postage stamps rather than in family albums. Someone to bow to rather than hug.

Luis wanted so much more from life than that.

He straightened up, dragging a hand over his face with a rasp of stubble. There was no point in going down that particular well-worn track again, he told himself wearily. It was strewn with landmines and it led only to places that were locked and barred to him.

To Emily, in other words.

In the hour that had elapsed since his father's body had been unhooked from its wires and tubes and the room had emptied of doctors and officials and palace staff, he had sat there alone, obsessively thinking over the possibilities like a prisoner exploring his cell for a means of escape.

There wasn't one, of course, he'd known that all along. But

he kept coming back to that thing she'd said last night on the beach, about him being king. *Do it your way*, she'd said. *You'll be brilliant.* Emily, who did everything passionately, wholeheartedly. Who couldn't pretend. Whom he loved and admired and trusted more than anyone else in the world.

He got to his feet, swaying slightly, his heart beating very hard. On the bed the figure of his father lay, already as cold and pale as an effigy on a tomb, but as if to prove a point, his own body fizzed and pulsed with energy and adrenaline. Quickly he took his father's lifeless hand and held it for a moment, and then he walked to the door without looking back.

The guards outside jerked to attention as he passed, shooting each other uneasy glances as he headed straight for the lift. The doors slid open and he punched the button for the ground floor. At that moment Tomás appeared in the doorway of the room opposite, an expression of alarm on his face.

'Your Highness! I mean…Your Majesty! Where are you—?'

The doors began to close. Realising that Luis had no intention of stopping them, Tomás made it into the lift just in time.

'Sir, what are you *doing*?'

His tone was a mixture of incredulity and disapproval, laced with pure panic. By contrast Luis was icy calm.

'Going back to the palace.'

'B-but the press are out there, sir. They're waiting for statements and photographs, and the suit I brought for you is still—'

Ruthlessly Luis cut through the details. 'I need to speak to Emily.'

'Ah.' It was a swift, defeated exhalation, but immediately Tomás drew himself up, visibly preparing to deliver bad news. 'I'm afraid Miss Balfour is returning to England, sir. I spoke to Josefina just a moment ago. She had a meeting with her this morning, after which it appears Miss Balfour's father arrived, quite by coincidence. In view of everything that's happened it seems that Miss Balfour has decided to go home.'

The lift came to a halt and Luis's lip curled into a sneer of contempt. 'Miss Balfour decided that, or Josefina did?' he asked, moving towards the door.

'Wait.' With uncharacteristic vehemence Tomás pressed the button to close the doors, and kept his hand there. 'It's too *late*, sir,' he said desperately. 'The helicopter is being prepared for take-off right now. By the time you get through the crowd outside and back to the palace she'll be gone. So why don't you go back upstairs and change into the suit and—'

He didn't get any further. The lift shook as, in one lightning-swift movement, Luis lunged at him grasping him by the collar and holding him up against the wall.

'No.' It was a low, savage growl. 'I will not wait, and I will not go back and get changed because I don't care about wearing the correct clothes or saying the correct thing. I never have, and if I'm going to do this thing…' His voice cracked a little, but he gritted his teeth and carried on. 'If I'm going to play this role for the rest of my life, I've got to do it *my* way. I've got to be *myself*—not my father or brother— and if people don't like it that's tough. But I can't just go through the motions any more. And I can't—'

He stopped, letting Tomás go and turning away.

'Sir?'

'I can't do it unless she's with me too.' Raising his arm Luis leaned briefly against the wall in an attitude of utter despair. 'Do you understand?'

There was a long pause. Then, very tentatively, Tomás reached out and put his hand on Luis's bunched, rigid shoulder. 'Yes,' he said so quietly it was almost a sigh. 'Yes, I think so.'

Luis raised his head and for a moment their eyes met, but then the lift doors were opening and through the glass front of the building they could see the crowd of people that had gathered to wait for news—camera crews, reporters, paparazzi—all unusually subdued by the grimness of the situation. The reception area was filled with palace security, who looked surprised and flustered by the unexpected appearance of the new King. There was a flurry of uneasy bowing.

With just the barest of nods Luis walked through them all to the doors. Following him, Tomás's face was drained of colour and covered in a sickly sheen of perspiration and he signalled a look of panic to the bodyguards.

Outside it took a moment for what was happening to filter through the crowd, and a ripple of feverish excitement disturbed the sombre mood as everyone pressed forward to get a glimpse of the new King—ashen with exhaustion, shirtless and in surf shorts. Security had gone into discreet overdrive and they held the crowd back as Luis went up to the small dais.

He hesitated for a moment, looking down and clearing his throat before speaking. 'I'm sorry to have to announce the death of my father, King Marcos Fernando,' he said slowly, pausing again as the gathered crowd gave a muted groan. 'He suffered a stroke in the early hours of this morning, and never regained consciousness. He died very peacefully just after 2:00 p.m.'

There was a moment of dead calm, and then a forest of microphones went up and questions rose in a deafening crescendo. But Luis simply held up his hands and, shaking his head, turned away. Striding over to the cordon he looked over the heads of the reporters pressed against it, to the back where the paparazzi lurked on motorbikes waiting to tail his car. A moment later there was uproar and confusion as Luis slipped beneath the cordon and into the crowd.

Security guards surged forwards from nowhere, barking instructions while Tomás, almost passing out with panic, tried to follow. But the hardened, cynical reporters had parted to let their king through and then swallowed him up completely so it was impossible to reach him. In seconds Luis found himself at the back of the press pack, camera flashes exploding like fireworks as he headed straight to the paparazzi photographer on the biggest, most powerful motorbike.

'How would you feel about being the first paparazzi in history to be decorated for services to the king?'

Finally fighting his way to the back of the crowd a few

moments later Tomás was just in time to see Luis climb onto
the bike. Swiftly, grimly, he shook hands with the photographer
before starting the engine with a roar. He wasn't wearing a
helmet, and as he accelerated away with a squeal of tyres there
was no mistaking the expression of desperate, haunted bleakness on his face.

'Is that everything?'

Oscar picked up the small case, frowning at how light it was,
and Emily looked around the beautiful suite for the last time.

'That's everything,' she said in a small voice. Everything that
belonged to her anyway. She was wearing the blue dress she'd
worn when they went to dinner with Luciana, but other than that
all the clothes Luis had ordered for her were still in the dressing
room. Not that the Duchess de Mesa would need any help with
her wardrobe, Emily thought bleakly. After all, she had qualified
for the job of Luis's wife on the grounds of having the perfect
image already. Maybe Luciana's nannies would get to use them.

Oh, God. Luciana. The thought of leaving her was like
knives in her flesh. The hour Emily had spent with her earlier,
maintaining a mask of cheerful reassurance that she'd see her
very soon and talking about all the things they would do when
she came over to England to visit, had left her drained, shaky
and feeling sick. It was some comfort that Valentina's maternity leave had come to an end, and with it Senhora Costa's
sterile rule in the nursery. It was a very different Luciana who
tearfully hugged her goodbye to the one who had greeted her
with such rigid shyness two months ago.

The helicopter was waiting on the lawn, and with every step
she took towards it Emily felt her heart crack wider open. Oscar
helped her into the back, settling her in as solicitously as if she
was ill, holding her hand as the blades started up and they rose
into the air. Emily watched as the palace grew smaller beneath
them and had to snatch her hand from Oscar's and press it
across her mouth to muffle the sobs she couldn't control.

'Oh, darling girl, I can't tell you how much I've longed to have you back,' Oscar said sadly. 'But not like this. Not with your heart broken. Tell me what happened.'

'I fell in love with him,' she whispered, leaning her head back and letting the tears fall down her cheeks. 'I knew it was dangerous, but I couldn't stop myself.'

'And he doesn't feel the same?'

'No.' She turned her face to the window and looked out over the treetops. It felt like her heart was being wrenched out of her chest as she saw the slate roof of *La Guarita* below. 'For him it was practical. It was *PR*,' she sobbed. 'And although in the end I desperately want to think that he did come to feel something for me it just wasn't enough. It wasn't *love*.'

Ahead, beyond the trees she could see the glitter of the sea. In a moment they would be flying over the beach where they'd danced last night, and where she'd woken up this morning in his arms. And then that would be it. Santosa would be behind them, and nothing but half a world of cold, deep ocean ahead. She closed her eyes, wondering how to get through the pain.

'You're sure about that?' Oscar asked gently. 'You're absolutely sure?'

'I'm sure,' she whispered. 'But even if I wasn't, doesn't that say something? I couldn't live like that…with someone who couldn't say it. I couldn't live not knowing…'

'No, sweetheart, you couldn't.' Oscar sighed. 'You need—'

He stopped abruptly, midsentence, and Emily opened her eyes.

'Daddy, what's wrong?'

Oscar was staring out of the window, his brow creased into a frown. Heart thudding, Emily followed his gaze.

Below them the tide was out and the beach was a wide, white expanse. Already the tents had been taken down and the ashes of the fire had been covered over, leaving no trace of last night's party. It was deserted, apart from a single figure.

A lone surfer, she thought dully, noticing the shorts, the bare, bronzed back and broad shoulders. He was bent over, as if he was looking for something in the sand, but moving quickly so that the muscles of his back rippled in the sun.

And then she realised. He wasn't looking.

He was writing.

Big letters in the sand—a message that she read incredulously through a mist of tears.

EMILY…I LOVE YOU.

She gave a desperate, incredulous sob, scrubbing the tears from her eyes so she could read it again, to make sure she wasn't wrong. And as she did so the tanned, bare-chested man on the beach heard the helicopter and straightened up, tipping his head back. And she saw that it really was Luis, and that he wore an expression of torment that matched her own.

'I was going to say you need someone who can tell you that they love you,' Oscar said in a voice that was choked with emotion. 'But I think that writing it in metre-high letters is even better.'

Her heart had risen up into her throat and was beating there, as if it might choke her. She opened her mouth to speak but no words came out. It didn't matter. Oscar was already leaning into the front of the cockpit and asking the pilot to land.

The sand swirled upwards as the helicopter came down, the wind from the blades ruffling Luis's dark gold hair as he stood, taut and unmoving in the centre of the storm, his head tipped back in an attitude of silent suffering, his perfect face mask-like. Throwing open the door Emily jumped down, her blue dress billowing up around her thighs, her eyes never leaving him.

Slowly, like a sleepwalker, she went towards him, stumbling slightly as her feet sank into the sand, pausing to kick off her shoes and then stopping altogether a few feet from him as she saw that his face was wet with tears.

'Oh, Luis…' she said in anguish. 'Your father. I'm so sorry.'

He gave a curt, dismissive shake of his head, as if her compassion flayed him. Everything about him resisted approach and despite the tears he looked terrifyingly, fiercely remote. 'I listened to what you said,' he growled in a voice like rusty razor blades. 'I'm going to try to do it my way. Be honest. Not hide anything. Do things from the heart.' He made a sweeping gesture to the message in the sand. 'Telling you I love you seemed like the most important place to start.'

A cry was torn from her throat and in an instant she had crossed the distance between them and he was opening his arms to her with a muffled groan of agonized surrender. As he folded her against his hard, hot body she could smell the musky scent of his damp skin and feel his heart smashing against his chest.

'The only problem is I don't know where to go from here,' he muttered through gritted teeth, cradling her cheek with his palm. 'I don't know how to carry on if you're not there to show me.'

'I'm here,' she gasped, reaching up to find his mouth, pressing hers against it. 'I'm here, I'm *here*.'

He kissed her back, wildly and hungrily, as if to prove that she was real. 'I'm not asking you to stay,' he rasped, breaking away and burying his face in her hair. 'I can't do that to you. But neither could I let you leave without knowing how much I love you.' He took her face between his hands and tilted it up towards him, so she was staring into his blazing golden eyes. 'I wanted you to know that I don't care about what the public think or what the papers say—I'll love you whatever you do and wherever you are, and I'll keep loving you in public and in private every minute of every day for the rest of my life.'

'I don't want to leave,' she said in a broken whisper. 'I don't want to leave you, ever again, but it's not that simple, is it? You're King now—that means you have a duty to Santosa, and a public image to maintain and—'

He stopped her with another furious kiss. 'I want my duty to be to you and our children before anything else,' he said angrily. 'I want my image to be of a man who, above all, is desperately, ridiculously in love with his beautiful wife. But I'm trying to give up being selfish so I don't know if I can ask—'

'Try,' she said fiercely. 'Oh, Luis, please *try*.'

'Oh, Emily…' he sighed, letting her go and taking a step back. Smiling crookedly he picked up the stick that he had dropped onto the sand. 'Close your eyes and let me finish the message.'

Half laughing, half sobbing, she did as she was told. From a distance away, above the sound of the wind and the waves, Luis's voice reached her, wrapping itself around her and making her shiver with love and longing.

'Emily Balfour, if I promise to show you every day how much I love you…' he shouted across the sand. 'If I swear never to put protocol…or obligation…or any stupid, outdated ideas of what I should *be* and *do* before your happiness…or let anyone tell us how we should live and bring up the many children I want to have with you…would you really be mad enough to do this?'

He broke off and she opened her eyes. He was standing a little distance away, and stretching away from him on the sand were the words *MARRY ME*.

She couldn't speak. Her throat closed up against the wild, racking sob of relief and joy and agonising, exquisite love that gathered there, so instead she extended one bare foot, pointing her toe and writing her answer in the damp sand as tears dripped down her face

YES.

And then she was running towards him and he caught her in his arms and gathered her to him, lifting her high. She wrapped her legs around his waist, her fingers twining in his tangled hair and he held her tightly against him as their mouths met. They kissed, on and on, oblivious to the wind whipping her hair across Luis's bare shoulders and the waves breaking behind them, to Oscar waiting, damp-eyed, beside the helicopter and the paparazzi photographers and news crews beginning to gather at the top of the dunes.

And this time there was no need for statements from the press office or quotes from palace sources. The figures locked together on the beach, the writing in the sand, told the whole story.

HARLEQUIN *Presents*

Coming Next Month

from **Harlequin Presents® EXTRA.** Available October 12, 2010.

#121 POWERFUL GREEK, HOUSEKEEPER WIFE
Robyn Donald
The Greek Tycoons

#122 THE GOOD GREEK WIFE?
Kate Walker
The Greek Tycoons

#123 BOARDROOM RIVALS, BEDROOM FIREWORKS!
Kimberly Lang
Back in His Bed

#124 UNFINISHED BUSINESS WITH THE DUKE
Heidi Rice
Back in His Bed

Coming Next Month

from **Harlequin Presents®.** Available October 26, 2010.

#2951 THE PREGNANCY SHOCK
Lynne Graham
The Drakos Baby

#2952 SOPHIE AND THE SCORCHING SICILIAN
Kim Lawrence
The Balfour Brides

#2953 FALCO: THE DARK GUARDIAN
Sandra Marton
The Orsini Brothers

#2954 CHOSEN BY THE SHEIKH
Kim Lawrence and Lynn Raye Harris

#2955 THE SABBIDES SECRET BABY
Jacqueline Baird

#2956 CASTELLANO'S MISTRESS OF REVENGE
Melanie Milburne

LARGER-PRINT BOOKS!

HARLEQUIN *Presents*~

PASSION
GUARANTEED
SEDUCTION

GET 2 FREE LARGER-PRINT NOVELS PLUS 2 FREE GIFTS!

YES! Please send me 2 FREE LARGER-PRINT Harlequin Presents® novels and my 2 FREE gifts (gifts are worth about $10). After receiving them, if I don't wish to receive any more books, I can return the shipping statement marked "cancel". If I don't cancel, I will receive 6 brand-new novels every month and be billed just $4.55 per book in the U.S. or $5.24 per book in Canada. That's a saving of at least 13% off the cover price! It's quite a bargain! Shipping and handling is just 50¢ per book.* I understand that accepting the 2 free books and gifts places me under no obligation to buy anything. I can always return a shipment and cancel at any time. Even if I never buy another book, the two free books and gifts are mine to keep forever.

176/376 HDN E5NG

Name _____ (PLEASE PRINT)

Address _____ Apt. #

City _____ State/Prov. _____ Zip/Postal Code

Signature (if under 18, a parent or guardian must sign)

Mail to the **Harlequin Reader Service:**
IN U.S.A.: P.O. Box 1867, Buffalo, NY 14240-1867
IN CANADA: P.O. Box 609, Fort Erie, Ontario L2A 5X3

Not valid for current subscribers to Harlequin Presents Larger-Print books.

Are you a subscriber to Harlequin Presents books and want to receive the larger-print edition? Call 1-800-873-8635 today!

* Terms and prices subject to change without notice. Prices do not include applicable taxes. Sales tax applicable in N.Y. Canadian residents will be charged applicable provincial taxes and GST. Offer not valid in Quebec. This offer is limited to one order per household. All orders subject to approval. Credit or debit balances in a customer's account(s) may be offset by any other outstanding balance owed by or to the customer. Please allow 4 to 6 weeks for delivery. Offer available while quantities last.

Your Privacy: Harlequin Books is committed to protecting your privacy. Our Privacy Policy is available online at www.eHarlequin.com or upon request from the Reader Service. From time to time we make our lists of customers available to reputable third parties who may have a product or service of interest to you. If you would prefer we not share your name and address, please check here. ☐

Help us get it right—We strive for accurate, respectful and relevant communications. To clarify or modify your communication preferences, visit us at www.ReaderService.com/consumerschoice.

HARLEQUIN®

A Romance

FOR EVERY MOOD™

Spotlight on

Inspirational

Wholesome romances
that touch the heart and soul.

See the next page
to enjoy a sneak peek from
the Love Inspired® Suspense
inspirational series.

*See below for a sneak peek from
our inspirational line, Love Inspired® Suspense*

*Enjoy this heart-stopping excerpt from
RUNNING BLIND
by top author Shirlee McCoy,
available November 2010!*

*The mission trip to Mexico was supposed to be an
adventure. But the thrill turns sour when Jenna Dougherty
and her roommate Magdalena are kidnapped.*

"It's okay. I'm here to help." The voice was as deep as the
darkness, but Jenna Dougherty didn't believe the lie. She
could do nothing but lie still as hands slid down her arms,
felt the rope around her wrists.

"I'm going to use a knife to cut you free, Jenna. Hold
still."

The cold blade of a knife pressed close to her head before
her gag fell away.

"I—" she started, but her mouth was dry, and she could
do nothing but suck in air.

"Shhh. Whatever needs to be said can be said when
we're out of here." Nick spoke quietly, his hand gentle on
her cheek. There and gone as he sliced through the ropes on
her wrists and ankles.

He pulled her upright. "Come on. We may be on
borrowed time."

"I can't leave my friend," Jenna rasped out.

"There's no one here. Just us."

"She has to be here." Jenna took a step away.

"There's no one here. Let's go before that changes."

"It's dark. Maybe if we find a light…"

"What did you say?"

"We need to turn on the light. I can't leave until I know that—"

"What can you see, Jenna?"

"Nothing."

"No shadows? No light?"

"No."

"It's broad daylight. There's light spilling in from the window I climbed in through. You can't see it?"

She went cold at his words.

"I can't see anything."

"You've got a nasty bruise on your forehead. Maybe that has something to do with it." His fingers traced the tender flesh on her forehead.

"It doesn't matter *how* it happened. I'm blind!"

Can Nick help Jenna find her friend or will chasing this trail have Jenna running blindly again into danger?

Find out in RUNNING BLIND, available in November 2010 only from Love Inspired Suspense.

SHLISEXP1110

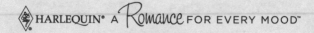